the truth about Cats and Wolves

ALETHEA KONTIS

Sugar Skull Books LLC

The Truth About Cats and Wolves
A Nocturne Falls Universe Story
Copyright © 2017 by Alethea Kontis

Cover design by Keri Knutson
Print Layout by Polgarus Studio

Dear Reader,

Nocturne Falls has become a magical place for so many people, myself included. Over and over I've heard from you that it's a town you'd love to visit and even live in! I can tell you that writing the books is just as much fun for me.

With your enthusiasm for the series in mind – and your many requests for more books – the Nocturne Falls Universe was born. It's a project near and dear to my heart, and one I am very excited about.

I hope these new, guest-authored books will entertain and delight you. And best of all, I hope they allow you to discover some great new authors! (And if you like this book, be sure to check out the rest of the Nocturne Falls Universe offerings.)

For more information about the Nocturne Falls Universe, visit http://kristenpainter.com/sugar-skull-books/

In the meantime, happy reading!

Kristen Painter

To all the extraordinary individuals who have ever donned a costume on Labor Day weekend in Georgia and walked with me in the parade.

You know who you are.

"Love…love takes time."

—Ivy Kincaid Merrow, *The Werewolf Meets His Match*

"To flaming youth let virtue be as wax,
And melt in her own fire: proclaim no shame
When the compulsive ardour gives the charge,
Since frost itself as actively doth burn
And reason panders will."

—*Hamlet*, Act III, Scene IV

1

"Are you sure this was the best choice?"

"Does it matter? At least I was given a choice. The only wrong decision would have been not making one." Kai Xanthopoulos stopped what she was doing and froze. Took a deep breath. She had to knead the dough gently for it to come out right, not pummel it into oblivion.

Thanks to Owen's insistence on discussing this topic again, she really, *really* wanted to pummel it into oblivion.

Kai dusted her palms with flour and patiently rolled the dough out into a long, snakey tube. "When the children in my family turn sixteen, they are allowed to get a job that has nothing to do with the restaurant business. I chose Delaney's Delectables. End of story."

"And when they're thirteen, children in your family also usually know what their powers are."

Another topic Kai loathed: her complete failure when it came to magic…beyond being able to have this conversation with Owen, that is. For a while, she suspected that Owen might be her familiar and that her powers would turn out to be witch-like in nature. But said powers—whatever their nature—still remained dormant.

"So what?" said Kai.

"So…I'm just saying, you might need a bit of guidance," said the cat. "I'm a fabulous guidance counselor."

"Yeah, I'll bet," Kai said dubiously. The only guidance Owen ever gave included suggestions that inevitably made *his* life better. "I'm a late bloomer. It's happened before. What, you think if I turn out to be a naiad or a marsh witch I'll ruin the candy? Or I'll lose it completely and start making a house out of gingerbread?"

"I'm being serious, Kai. If you had stayed at the diner, you could have been a manager. Here you're just a…"

"Cook? Servant? Dogsbody?" Kai punctuated the last word with a grin. If Owen was going to push all her buttons today, she was going to push right back.

Out of the corner of her eye, she saw Owen make a face. "Essentially. Your yiayia's a baker, Kai. Not you. You don't even like sweets."

Her melted butter had separated, so she used the paintbrush to stir it up a bit. "Doesn't mean I'm not awesome at making them. And I do like sweets. I like chocolate."

Owen sighed. "Everybody likes chocolate. *Normal* chocolate. You only like that dark, bitter stuff. With acorns in it."

One laugh burst out of Kai but she held the rest back. Owen always made her laugh when they were arguing; undoubtedly why she indulged him with these ridiculous discussions. "They're called hazelnuts, moron. Food of the gods."

Owen made a noise like a game show buzzer and hopped up on the counter to watch her work. "Wrong. Anchovies. *Those* are the food of the gods."

"Riiiight. If I was a naiad, maybe. Or a cat." Kai painted the butter onto the dough-snake with one hand. She used the other hand to liberally sprinkle it with a mix of cinnamon and sugar. The actions helped her mind focus beyond the verbal sparring, on the message Owen was actually trying to convey to her.

"Oh. Mygosh." Kai lifted the buttery brush and pointed it at Owen. "*J'accuse.*"

Owen's pale green eyes shifted away from her level gaze. He was suddenly very interested in everything in the sweet shop that wasn't her. Kai suspected that if the cat had been able to whistle innocently, this was the moment he would have done it. "I have no idea what you're talking about."

"This has nothing to do with me! If I'm not at the diner looking out for you, then the quality of your dumpster diving is severely diminished."

"I'm a carnivore, Kai. The best you can offer me here is a fallen cake."

Exasperated, Kai tossed the brush back into the butter and began twisting the cinnamon dough-snake in, out, and around itself. "No one's forcing you to be here, Owen."

"But, Kai, my darling…" His tone of voice had completely shifted. *Now* he was going to try and warm up to her? No way.

"Enough. I have work to do. Out." Owen didn't budge. Kai snapped her fingers. "You shouldn't even be in here. And you definitely shouldn't be on the counter. Are you *trying* to get me fired?" She snapped her fingers again and pointed at the door. "Out!"

In his own time, Owen yawned and lazily leapt off the counter, as if leaving were something he'd meant to do all along. He sauntered toward the front door, just in time for a woman to open it for him. The bells tinkled like a fairy's laugh. "We're not finished, Kalliope," he said as he walked away.

"We're finished for today!" Kai yelled after him, and then realized how ridiculous she sounded. She closed her eyes and took another deep breath to calm herself. When she opened them up again, she was face to face with Verity Mercer.

"I have lots of friends who talk to their cats, but…girl, you take the cake." She waved her hand to indicate the refrigerated case full of beautifully decorated cakes beside them. "So to speak."

"Oh, wow." Kai felt her face flush. She'd always been a terrible blusher, but the embarrassment of being caught in mid-debate with a cat—by a human, no less—set her cheeks burning. "I am *so* sorry, Ms. Mercer. It will never happen again, I promise."

Verity Mercer was one of Roxy St. James's writers-in-residence. Roxy, a bestselling novelist herself, had fixed up her guest house for the express purpose of inviting her friends to Nocturne Falls for writing retreats. Roxy also happened to be the shop owner's best friend, Mrs. Delaney Ellingham Herself.

Ms. Mercer must have recognized Kai's obvious distress, because she moved to the pitcher on the counter and poured Kai a cup of water. "Now, sweetie. Don't fret. Delaney will never know your cat was in here…well, not from me, anyway. And please, call me Verity."

"Yes, Miss Verity. Thank you." She gulped the water down, hoping it would go straight to her flaming cheeks. With her face like this and her unruly brown curls constantly trying to escape from her bun, she must look like a harpy. Not exactly the "delectable" appearance Delaney Ellingham would have wanted of her hired help. Kai had such a short fuse lately…it seemed like everything was setting her off. Especially Owen. "He's not my cat anyway. He doesn't belong to anyone, least of all me. He's just a stray that hangs around the diner."

"Really?" Verity raised an eyebrow. "Could have fooled me."

"My parents aren't into pets," said Kai.

"Well, I must say, for a stray, that is one well-groomed pixie cat."

Kai wet a napkin with the water and put it on the back of her neck. "Is that what breed he is? My little sister calls him Alien Cat."

"What do you call him?"

Kai shrugged. "Owen, the Pain in My Neck."

"Seems like a fine title. Ooh, what are you making?" She pointed to the glistening, serpentine mounds of dough. "They look kind of…"

"Disgusting?" Kai offered.

"Well, yes, if I'm being honest."

"Perfect! That's what I was going for. Miss Delaney said that I was welcome to experiment when there weren't any customers and this is my creation. Aren't they brilliant?"

"What *are* they?" Verity asked skeptically.

Kai leaned in to share the secret. "Sweetbreads," she whispered. "Get it?"

Verity put her hands on her hips and furrowed her brow.

"Technically it's just Monkey Bread," said Kai. "I tried to make them in the shape of a pancreas or a heart, but they just came out like giant thick blobs, so I decided to go the lumpy-intestine route. They'll cook more evenly this way too. I thought they'd be the perfect thing to sell in the shop during the Scaresgiving Parade." Now Verity was staring at her. "You think it's a terrible idea."

"No, I agree with you," said Verity. "They're positively brilliant. In this fabulous town full of Halloween-crazed nutballs, the tourists are going to be eating these up. Literally!"

Kai clapped her hands together in a puff of flour. "Really? You think so?"

"I do," said Verity. "And I look forward to sampling this first batch. You go pop those in the oven, and I'll set up over here. Is that all right?"

Kai nodded. Verity often came into town to write. Roxy's guest house was cozy enough, but the costumed residents and visitors inspired her, she said. The random splashes of color and cheeriness "pleased her Muse." Little did she know that most of those costumes weren't costumes at all.

Verity Mercer was a guest in this town, and human, and therefore not privy to the fact that all of Roxy's friends and neighbors who spent their days acting like gargoyles and witches and werewolves were *actually* gargoyles and witches and werewolves. As long as Verity kept drinking the local enchanted water, she'd be none the wiser. So Kai kept her mouth shut and delivered a fresh glass of water to Verity's table. As far as Verity knew, Kai was just a crazy teenager who talked to cats.

She would never know that Kai heard this cat talk back.

Kai slid the cookie sheet in the oven and then stopped in the bathroom to wash her hands and splash some water on her face. She took off her flour-covered apron and changed into a fresh one. She felt much more composed when she walked back out to the sales floor. "I'm going to check the sweetbreads in about fifteen minutes," she said to Verity. "Can I get you anything in the meantime? Besides water?"

"A coffee would be great," Verity said into her laptop, her fingers already flying across the keys.

"The usual?" asked Kai.

"Mmm-hmm."

Kai walked to the front door and stood by the clear glass. Nocturne Falls was a year-round tourist destination, and Black Cat Boulevard was one of the main drags…but for some reason, this sunny Wednesday afternoon was deader than usual. There was no traffic on the road or cars parked in the street, just Verity's sea-foam-green Vespa on the sidewalk. For the first time in a very long time, Nocturne Falls looked like an actual ghost town. With no ghosts in it whatsoever.

It also meant that Bellamy would be bored to tears.

Kai waved her arms, trying to get her bestie's attention. She could have abandoned her post for five minutes and walked across the street, but communicating from one store picture window to another was so much more fun.

Bellamy had her elbows planted on the counter of Hallowed Bean, head in her hands, wings drooping sadly at her back. It was not the fairy who noticed Kai's wild gesturing but Maya and Kaley, the teen witches who just so happened to be sitting at a table right by the window.

Kai smiled, waved, and pointed to Bellamy. She could have texted, but she wasn't supposed to have her phone on at work.

Maya and Kaley waved back. Maya walked to the counter and said something to Bellamy, who perked up immediately and ran to the window.

Kai pointed to Verity, even though Bellamy couldn't see her, and then pantomimed frantic typing.

Bellamy also pantomimed typing and giggled. She made a sign for drinking.

Kai nodded, and then held up two fingers, placing an order for both Verity and herself. Unless some miracle occurred in the next couple of hours, there wouldn't be many more customers today, which meant that the time would pass by incredibly slowly. A coffee would certainly help with that. Especially one made by Bellamy.

Bellamy nodded back cheerfully, the colorful

locks in her honey-blonde hair bobbing like a drunken rainbow. She gave Kai two thumbs up, did a little dance, and blew her a kiss.

And then a cloud went over the sun.

It was as if all the color drained from the world, and only a strange blue tint was left. Out of nowhere, the wind picked up. In the distance, Kai could hear sirens. A tornado in November? Totally not the right time of year. Besides, before a tornado the sky usually tinted green or yellow, not blue.

Without opening the door, Kai strained to look as far as she could down one end of the street, and then the other…and that's when she saw him. He tore out of the alleyway like a dark streak and sped down the middle of the boulevard. She heard a whistle now, and more sirens. This was bad news.

Keep running, she said inside her head. *Keep running. Don't stop here. There is nothing for you here.*

But he did stop. Dead in the middle of the street between Delaney's Delectables and Hallowed Bean. He put his hands on his knees to catch his breath. Chunks of long, black hair fell forward, covering his face.

Danger. She felt the word in every fiber of her being.

Kai looked to her friends at the window of Hallowed Bean. Maya was standing now; the chair where she'd been sitting had fallen over on its side. Kaley's eyes were wide, as if she wanted to scream, but Bellamy's hand was over her mouth.

The guy in the road stood up. Seemed to sniff the air.

Not them, Kai's inner voice went on. *If you need a place to hide, it's not there.*

He turned his head to stare right at Kai.

He was the most magnificent boy she'd ever seen. Man. Young man. Like a rock star. Or the son of a rock star. He was swathed in black: his hair, his jacket, his shirt, his jeans, his boots. As he came closer, Kai could tell that the boots were scuffed. The jeans and shirt were torn. The jacket was held together in places with safety pins. Closer. And closer.

He stalked to the door like a death wish.

Kai stepped back, but she could not look away from him. Would not. If he lost interest in her, he might go across the street and hurt her friends. She couldn't risk that.

His skin was deeply tan. His jaw was square and hard with a shadow of stubble. His nose was cut on the bridge. It might have been broken, and one eye looked like he'd been punched. His eyebrows were thick and shot with a streak of silver. All of this was framed by a mane of wavy, shoulder-length hair.

The bells tinkled as the door opened, but no one was laughing.

Kai stopped moving backward and stood her ground. His eyes were all she could see now. Gray and gold. Hunted. Haunted. The heel of his boot scraped against the polished hardwood floor as he stepped nearer. The air smelled like lightning.

Verity wasn't tapping on her keyboard anymore, but Kai didn't dare look away from his eyes. He could have had a knife or a gun…but she couldn't look away. She heard muffled voices outside the shop: people running in the street, calling out to each other. A lot of people.

There's no escape for you, buddy, Kai's inner voice said. *Not in this town.*

He lifted a hand to her cheek—his knuckles were bloody—but Kai remained as still as stone. One corner of his mouth turned up in what might have been a smile...but before she could decide, he was kissing her.

He was kissing her and his lips felt soft and kind. He was kissing her and the whole world melted away to nothing. He was kissing her and her heart stopped beating. He was kissing her and warmth spread through her body, all the way down to her toes. He was kissing her...and she was pretty sure she was kissing him back...and it was *beautiful*. She had never felt so beautiful in her whole entire life.

She heard Bellamy's voice ring out in the street, signaling the search party, and it pulled her back to reality. She pushed at the stranger's exceptionally broad chest—all of it muscle—and he broke away without a struggle.

"Proclaim no shame," he whispered in her ear, his deep voice a cross between a growl and a touch.

The bells tinkled again, madly this time, again and again as the sweet shop filled with people. Sheriff Merrow took one side of the stranger and Deputy Blythe took the other. Together they pulled him to the door. Someone put a protective arm around Kai. Verity.

"Sanctuary!" the prisoner cried. "Sanctuary! Sanctuary!"

"I'll give you sanctuary, kid," said the sheriff. "Down at the station."

The rest of the crowd left with the prisoner, but Deputy Cruz stayed behind. "Kai, are you all right?"

That was the question, wasn't it? *Was* she all right? It had all happened so fast, and yet it wouldn't stop replaying itself in her mind. She wasn't sure she wanted it to.

"Let's give her a minute, deputy," Kai heard

Verity say. "She needs to collect herself. And her friends need to make sure she's okay."

Kai let Verity speak for her, because she didn't seem to be able to form sentences yet. Or words. The ones Verity was using seemed just fine.

Deputy Cruz nodded. "Take your time. Just send her down to the station as soon as she's ready."

"Yes, sir."

The bells tinkled again as the deputy left, but he didn't get far. Kai heard him ask Bellamy and Maya and Kaley for their statements.

"Honey, tell me the truth now. Are you okay?" Verity rolled her eyes. "What am I saying? That boy kissed you within an inch of your life. Of course you're not okay. My guess is right now you're torn between quite a lot of feelings. Am I right?"

Kai nodded. Her whole body felt like a fire doused by a bucket of water, leaving nothing behind but smoke and dying embers.

"What I want to know is, what did he say to you?"

"'Proclaim no shame,'" Kai repeated. Coming from her mouth, the words sounded flat and high-pitched. "What's that from?"

"Well," said Verity, "I don't pretend to know all the music you kids listen to these days, but back in my time that was a quote from *Hamlet*."

It made an odd sort of sense, seeing as what he'd yelled on his way out the door had been Quasimodo's famous line from *The Hunchback of Notre Dame*. That one, she did know.

Kai blinked into the daylight that seemed all too bright now. "What kind of delinquent runs from the police and kisses strange girls while quoting Shakespeare and Victor Hugo?"

"Oh, sweetie." Verity sighed and gave Kai a reassuring squeeze. "The very best kind."

2

Finn fought like a mad dog until the sheriff and his butch deputy threw him into the back of the squad car. When they pulled him back out again he resumed his struggle, with all the teeth and nails and dead weight he could manage…but not a word.

"Birdie," the sheriff barked. "Get the key and let Ned out of the cage."

The older woman at the desk shook her head, even as she was opening the drawer. "Are you positive? I'm not entirely sure he's sobered up yet."

The sheriff and his deputy dragged Finn before the dumpy, pasty-faced man that sat in what appeared to be the only cell this tiny town possessed. How quaint.

"Hey, Ned," said the sheriff. "Interested in sharing your space with this kid?"

Finn knew how rough he already looked. He bared his teeth and snarled for good measure.

"Not particularly," said Ned. He needed no more encouragement to slip out of the cell before the sheriff tossed Finn in. Finn caught a whiff of Ned as they passed each other—the man's clothes stank like a brewery, but there was no alcohol on his breath. If he had to guess, he'd have said the man had taken a bath in a beer and got himself locked up for a good night's sleep. Ned's missus was either pregnant or mad. Or both.

The sheriff turned the key in the cell's lock and slammed the bolt home. "Blythe here will drive you," he said to Ned. "I suggest you stop and buy some flowers for Anna Louise on the way. And maybe a clean shirt."

Finn sank to the floor in the most shadowed corner of the cell, but he grinned in the darkness.

The sheriff had smelled the same thing, then. Whether or not Hank Merrow was as great a wolf as his legend remained to be seen, but so far Finn was impressed.

The second deputy walked in just as the first one left with Ned.

"Cruz," said Hank, "I need you to go out there and make sure everyone that wants to has given a statement. Then let them know there's nothing more to see."

"Good luck with that," said the receptionist.

"Sure, boss," said Cruz. "What are we going to do with the kid?"

"I'm going to let him cool his jets while the dust settles. Birdie, can you get my wife on the phone?"

"Your wife is already here." A statuesque blonde walked in the front door.

Finn raised his head. The last time he'd seen Ivy, she'd been at least a foot shorter and a hell of a lot less gorgeous. But then, so had he. She smelled like cinnamon and fresh-baked bread and…mated. She smelled well and truly mated. She even looked happy, beneath the scowl and furrowed brow and everything. Finn squeezed his eyes shut and said another quick prayer that he'd come to the right place.

"Perfect timing, dear," said the receptionist.

The sheriff actually looked surprised. "How did you…? Where's Charlie?"

"Small town, baby." Ivy tossed her jacket on an empty chair and kissed her husband on the cheek. "Charlie's with Delaney at the sweet shop. We were at her house with Roxy when Verity called."

"What did she tell you?" asked Birdie.

"More than my husband here knows, I'll wager. Enough for me to want to come see for myself. Is that the wolf?"

"You know he's a wolf?" asked Hank.

Birdie narrowed her eyes at Ivy. "That Verity must be one heck of a storyteller."

"I had my suspicions," said Ivy. "Until I walked in this door and smelled it for sure. Don't worry, Verity's still oblivious. He give you a name yet?"

"No." Hank gestured to the cell. "Remind you

of anyone?" he asked playfully.

Ivy pinned her husband with a look. "Very funny."

Hank grinned. "I'll just let you see for yourself."

Finn fought the urge to shrink into the corner as Ivy's footsteps crossed the floor. He'd come this far, no sense in turning tail now. Finn let the fear build up inside him. It filled his soul and stayed there, steeping into his particular brand of riotous, ridiculous, reckless rebellion. It was a stupid way to be brave. But it was all he had.

Ivy stopped at the bars and stared into his shadows. "Hey," she called to him. When Finn didn't respond, she turned to her husband. "Has he said anything at all?"

"Not since we arrested him. As we pulled him out of the shop he called for sanctuary. Is that even a thing?"

Ivy froze at Hank's words and Finn's heart soared. She *did* remember. Maybe there was hope for him yet. "How many times did he say it?" she asked in a low tone.

"Three times," said Hank, but Ivy already knew the answer.

She wrapped her fingers around the bars and called gently into the shadows once more. "Finn?"

Finn wanted to leap at the bars and hug Ivy. He wanted to collapse in her arms and break down like the little boy he used to be and tell her everything, the entire mess he'd gotten mixed up in, all the things that weren't his fault...and all the things that were. She would understand. She'd crept under the bed with him when he was small and hiding from Pappy Harlan. She'd stayed there all night and held his hand, no questions asked, and in the morning they'd never spoken of it again. Ivy knew because her pa was just as bad. They might have been born a decade apart on different branches of the Kincaid family tree, but they were still the same inside.

And yet, when he stood and stepped out of the shadows, that festering pot of fear inside him bubbled over and what came out of his mouth was a smarmy, "Looking good, cuz."

For a moment, the defiant eyes he stared into were not Ivy's but the deep olive brown of the girl's in the sweet shop. The hairs at the back of his neck stood on end. For half a second, Finn forgot the trouble he was in. In the next half-second, disappointment washed over Ivy's face and it all sunk in again.

Hank sneered. "One of the Tennessee brats, right? I should have known."

Finn tried to be honest, without sounding pathetic, so he opted for anger. "You told me that I could always come to you and call for sanctuary. Well, I need it now."

"Oh, Finn." Ivy closed her eyes. "Sanctuary is a dream. A lycan fairy tale told to wolf cubs in an effort to keep them from turning into Omegas. Sometimes pups will try harder, risk more, if they think there's a way out. And you were so scared…"

It was Finn's turn to be disappointed. The anger was real now. "There's no such thing as sanctuary?"

Hank shook his head. "There might have been, hundreds of years ago, but no pack would recognize that now. If you called 'Sanctuary' at a tribunal, they'd just laugh in your face."

Finn turned away from Hank, as if that small gesture could make the harsh words he'd spoken disappear. "So you lied."

"I told a story to a little boy because I thought it would keep him safe," said Ivy. "And it did."

"Until now." Finn fell to one knee and bowed before Hank. "Fine. I forfeit all ties to Tennessee and pledge myself to the Georgia Pack. Got a knife?"

"Not one I give to prisoners," Hank said sternly.

"Hank's not the Alpha anyway," said Ivy. "His dad is. But even if he was, babe, it doesn't work like that."

Ivy's term of endearment only served to remind Finn that he was as young and powerless as he felt. "Why not?" He swallowed the desperation in his throat with a growl. "*You* did it."

"My marriage was arranged to broker a peace

between the packs."

Was Ivy actually buying her own crap? "Your marriage was a sham set up by your old man," he spat. "But you made it work. And then you got your son *and* your little brother out. All I'm asking is to be let out too." Finn wrapped his fingers over hers and bared his soul. "Ivy, please."

"*Ahem.*" Birdie's interruption startled Finn enough that he snatched his hand away from Ivy's and stepped back from the bars. "It seems to me that you young'uns are going about this all wrong." She crossed her arms over her ample bosom and tapped her long, red nails against her elbow. "For starters, you're getting this story all out of order."

"Aunt Birdie's right." Ivy crossed her arms as well. "What sort of trouble are you in, Finn?"

Finn clenched his jaw determinedly.

"No, no, no." Birdie flapped her hands in the air. "It's too late for that now. Let's deal with the more immediate situation, shall we? This town wants gossip. That tall glass of trouble over there caused quite the scene to get Hank's attention, so we're going to have to give those people some sort of story, and soon. The actual wolves can wait until we're done with the virtual ones outside."

Hank counted the charges off on his fingers. "There's destruction of property and resisting arrest—"

"I just got off the phone with Carl, the owner of the newsstand," said Birdie. "Such a nice man. He's willing to drop the charges, provided he's compensated for the damage. Resisting arrest is your purview, nephew."

"Only for you, Birdie." Hank lifted a third finger. "But then there's assaulting a minor. That's a big one, kid. If Kai or her parents decide to press charges, there's nothing I can do to save you. No matter what pack you're from."

"Nor should you," said Ivy sternly. "What in the world got into you?"

Finn wished he could explain why he'd done what he'd done, if only to understand it himself. All he knew was that of all the stupid things he'd done in his life, this one didn't feel stupid at all. It felt *right*. Nothing in his life up until now had ever felt so right.

"Kai?" Birdie went from hen to hyena in the space of a second. "What does she have to do with all this?" She turned and unleashed her wrath on Finn. "If you harmed so much as a hair on that sweet girl's head, I will tear you limb from limb and I will take my time." Her voice became louder and screechier with each angry word. "Well? Answer me! What did you do to her, you little—"

"He kissed me," said a voice from the doorway.

"My, doesn't everyone have incredibly good timing today?" Birdie, eerily calm now, patted her hair…and then realized what Kai had said. "Wait. He what?"

Hank's nostrils flared. "He better be glad I missed that."

"Verity didn't miss it," said Ivy. "I imagine it will fill an entire chapter in her next book."

Finn only half-listened to their ramblings, waiting for the girl—Kai—to speak again. She'd taken off that ridiculous Halloween apron and let her hair down. It surrounded her face in a mahogany cloud. And those eyes…he hadn't misremembered them. They captured him in an intense stare that refused to be ignored.

No one spoke as she crossed to his cell. Hank and Ivy stepped away so that she could stand in front of Finn, so close that if he reached out he might be able to capture a strand of that thick mane. He inhaled slowly and deeply, trying not to make it obvious that he was breathing her in. She smelled like sugar and sweat and some kind of wildflower he'd forgotten the name of. The combination was intoxicating.

He knew as well as any wolf that the full moon was weeks away. There was no reason for these urges other than the ache in his chest and the deep pools of her eyes.

Why?

She hadn't spoken out loud, but he heard the word in his head just the same. The voice was warm embers in a banked fire, the same voice that had echoed in his mind when he'd stopped on the street to catch his breath. The tickle at the back of his neck spread down his spine.

He doesn't even know me. And it's not like I'm a supermodel or anything. So...why? Why kiss me? Why kiss anyone at all? He was obviously running away from some kind of trouble. If he'd only kept running, he might have escaped...

Finn's brow furrowed. If Kai had any inkling that he could hear her, she would have guarded her thoughts much better. How could someone have that much power and not know it? But now was not the time and place for such a private revelation, even though he could answer most of her questions. She *was* beautiful. She had surprised him, when he thought nothing in this world could have that effect on him anymore. He'd stopped running because his goal all along had been to get attention, not escape. Especially not now that he'd met her. He'd stay in this cell for ages if it meant he'd have the chance to know her better.

But he didn't say any of those things. And she obviously couldn't read his mind.

She let her lids fall over those mesmeric eyes, breaking the spell between them.

"We won't press charges," she said. "I'll talk to my parents."

Finn wiggled his ears. Her outer voice was so different from her inner voice, it was difficult rationalizing that they both came from the same person.

"Are you sure?" Hank asked.

Kai took Finn's measure from head to toe, sizing him up without meeting his eyes. "He's not worth it," she said with great disdain. "Am I free to go?"

"Free as a bird," said Hank. "Thanks for coming down, Kai."

As she turned to go, something silvery and metallic hit the floor. Kai's hand flew to her bare neck.

"I've got it." Birdie bent and picked up the delicate chain. "Here you go, sweetie. Come on. I'll walk you out."

"There's something about that girl…" said

Hank. As he watched Kai walk away, Finn agreed. But probably not about the same something Hank was referencing to.

"She's bold enough to bust a wolf's balls," said Ivy. "I like her. Is she one of us or one of them?" Finn could only assume she meant the human tourists and residents of this crazy burg.

"She's Greek," answered Hank.

"Ah," was all that Ivy said in response.

What did her nationality have to do with it? Inwardly, Finn cursed himself for living such a sheltered life in the wilds of Tennessee...not that he'd had much choice. Everything he knew about wolves, witches, and whatnot, he'd learned about in books. He'd ventured into the cities now and again, but he had very little firsthand experience with paranormals outside his family. Especially ones who walked the streets freely and discussed their natures like football teams.

"Okay then," Ivy said to her husband. "All the charges have been dropped. Go ahead and let him out of there."

Hank showed no sign that he was about to do any such thing. "We still don't know what he's done"—Hank gave Finn the side-eye—"beside destroying Carl's newsstand. And we don't know where he's going after this. He may be your cousin, but based on today's behavior, I don't exactly trust him."

Plus the fact that I'm a Kincaid, Finn thought but didn't say. He'd long since learned when to keep his mouth shut. And when to use it to piss off the largest amount of people in the smallest amount of time.

"What do you mean?" said Ivy. "He's coming home with us."

"What?" asked Finn.

"What?" yelled Hank.

"Just because our pack won't officially honor a fairy tale doesn't mean I can't." Ivy pointed to Finn. "I offered that child sanctuary, and I am honor bound to fulfill that promise. He can stay on the couch until we figure out what to do with him."

Finn braced himself. One didn't just throw the words "honor" and "promise" down in front of a future Alpha without risking life and limb. Finn had been beaten to a pulp for far less. Ivy too, probably. Finn searched Hank's face. It was obvious that Hank knew he was being manipulated.

And he *liked* it.

This was one crazy town all right.

Hank slid the key into the cell's lock. "You heard the woman, kid. A promise is a promise. Let's go." He smiled at his wife as he opened the door. Ivy smiled back and turned to retrieve her jacket.

Hank caught Finn's arm as he left the cell. "You cause any more trouble or bring danger onto me or my family, there won't be enough of you left to put back in this cage."

Finn sneered at the sheriff and yanked his arm out of that iron grip.

Oh, yeah. He'd definitely come to the right place.

3

"Did you see him?"

"Are you all right?"

"Did he say anything?"

"What happened to your necklace?"

"Is he really your boyfriend?"

"Seriously, Kai, are you okay?"

Kai could feel the heat rising up into her cheeks again. "Ohmigod, y'all. *Chill*. Not here."

For once, Bellamy and Maya and Kaley did as they were told. The trio closed ranks around Kai, acting as a buffer from the crowd gathered around the police station. Kai picked a direction and started walking, wishing the November air was a lot chillier. Her head was killing her. Maybe she was coming down with a cold. Maybe she'd caught something from that kiss. Maybe tall, dark, and handsome had been running from the CDC because he had a virulent strain of some horrible and contagious disease, and he'd given it straight to her.

Kai shook her head. She was being silly. Almost as silly as Birdie making up stories for the crowd outside the police station. And that had been quite an impressive feat in itself.

Everything Birdie had said from the moment they'd walked through the door onto the street was an out-and-out lie. She'd gone on jovially about "raging hormones" and "lovers spats" and "kids these days." Kai—who normally would have refuted all of that—just clutched her broken necklace in her fist and never said a word. She recognized a cover story when she heard one. It seemed that the longer a person lived in this town, the easier it was to lie to the masses. No matter how much magicked falls water the humans drank, some things in Nocturne Falls still needed explaining from time to time.

There are more things in heaven and earth, Horatio, than are dreamt of in your philosophy.

Kai frowned. Shakespeare again. And *Hamlet* again, if she wasn't mistaken. She was a science nerd, not some old world theatre geek. Why on "heaven and earth" was this nonsense running through her mind?

Suddenly she remembered his lips on hers again. The warmth of his hand cupping her face. The brush of his breath as he whispered in her ear. Her heart flipped in her chest. Her cheeks flushed a deeper hue. *That's* what was on her mind. That was the disease she'd caught: plain, old-fashioned lust.

And she didn't even know his name.

"Where are we goin'?" whispered Bellamy.

The fairy's delicate voice was enough to dispel Kai's brain fugue. "I...I don't know. You probably need to get back to the coffee shop, right?" Verity had said she'd look after the sweet shop until Delaney arrived, but Bellamy had just locked the door of Hallowed Bean and come running to the station.

"I'm good. I called Joan and gave her the short version. She told me to lock up and not worry a thing about it. The cops—and you—were far more important."

"You're the best, Bell." Bellamy's terminal optimism was part fairy nature and part personal awesome, and Kai would always love her for that. Kai turned to Maya and Kaley. "Seriously. I love all of you."

"We townies have to stick together," said Kaley.

Bellamy raised a finger, the one with the sky-blue painted nail. "But don't think you're gettin' off that easy."

"Yeah, chica," said Maya. "You have some serious 'splainin' to do."

"So where are we goin'?" Bellamy asked again.

"The diner," said Kai. "I have to tell my parents before they hear all this from someone else." In a town this small, everyone knew everyone else's business, no newspaper bulletin or social media required. Even if they couldn't see the future like her father could. Dad might know. Probably did know. But Kai's phone hadn't buzzed yet, which meant Mom was still in the dark.

"Good." Maya pushed Kai forward. "Talk on the way."

"I..." Kai suddenly found herself at a loss for words. "I don't know where to start. What exactly did y'all see?"

"No way," said Kaley. "This is your story."

"Tell us what it was like kissing that yummy hunk of man flesh," said Maya.

"Hush, you." Bellamy fake-punched Maya in the arm. "Start from the point where he stopped in the road. When the sky went dark."

"You noticed that too?" Kai asked. All three of the other girls nodded. "Did any of you have anything to do with that?" All three of them shook their heads. Curious. "Well...first of all, I'm pretty sure he's a wolf."

Bellamy stopped so short that Kai got a face full of wings. "Seriously?"

"Wasn't it obvious?" asked Kaley.

Kai wasn't surprised at the comment. Of course Kaley would have known—she could read auras. Too bad she couldn't read names and backstories as well.

"Lucky duck," Maya said jadedly.

Every girl at Harmswood knew about wolf-shifters. They were sexy, sexy beasts and they knew it. Even the less traditionally attractive ones. Especially during that time of the month. And on the full moon.

But the wolves all stayed pretty insular—ran in their own pack, as it were. They didn't give anyone outside their species much more than the time of day. That a wolf had come within three feet of Kai, never mind kissed her the way he had…well, it was impossible.

Except for the part where it had actually happened.

"What's his name?" asked Kaley. "Where's he from?"

"What did the cops want with him?" asked Maya.

"I don't know, and I don't know," Kai said to each in turn. "All I know is that he kissed me. Really kissed me, like in a movie. And Verity Mercer sat and watched the whole thing so I know it wasn't a dream. But wow..." Kai shivered, despite herself. "It sure felt like a dream."

Maya chuckled deviously. Bellamy and Kaley sighed in unison. Both exclamations pretty much covered how Kai felt herself.

"Honestly though," said Kaley, "I'm just glad he didn't kill you. 'Cause we were kind of afraid that's where it was headed."

"I was fixing to conjure one serious spell," said Maya. "The kind of spell I really don't like doing in the first place."

Bellamy took Kai's hand. "We were so worried for you, boo."

"I was worried too," said Kai. "Trust me. When he walked through that door I was so scared. All I could think was that I'd rather have him hurt me than all of you. I honestly have no idea why I didn't wet my pants right then and there." Thank goodness she hadn't. Was it possible that somehow, deep down, she had known he'd meant her no harm?

And yet…

There had been nothing safe about that kiss.

"So what are you goin' to do now?"

Bellamy was very good at asking questions Kai was already asking herself. Unfortunately, there was only one good answer.

"Nothing. There's nothing to do. He used me as the grand finale of some punk rebel statement. Statement's made. He's the sheriff's problem now. I'm going to forget about it, move on, and chalk it up to one of those crazy things that only happens in our town."

Kai could tell by her friends' silence that none of them believed her. That was okay. She didn't particularly believe herself much either. But she wasn't about to go chasing after that bad boy wolf like some crazy, lovestruck girl. Such things never ended well. Especially if the girl in hot pursuit wasn't a wolf herself.

Thankfully the trio didn't have much time to be disappointed that Kai wasn't going to kiss and tell, since they were already at the diner. She bid Bellamy, Maya, and Kaley farewell, then hugged Bellamy again when she came back for seconds. "Love you, Kai," the fairy whispered into her hair. "I'm so glad you're okay."

"Love you too, Bell. I'm glad we're all okay."

Kai stared up at Mummy's Diner and took a deep breath. For her entire sixteen-year-old existence, this place had been her second home. Kai's great-great grandfather escaped the Ottoman Empire during the Great Fire of Asia Minor, and then came to America and did what most Greeks did: went to work in a diner. A Xanthopoulos had worked in Mummy's Diner ever since that day…until Kai had chosen another path.

Reminded of her earlier discussion about that same subject—heavens, it felt like forever ago—Kai scanned the bushes around the diner for any sign of movement. There it was: a flash of light, curly fur. Seconds later, a narrow head and pointed ears stuck out from the leaves.

"Hey there, trouble. Come crawling back to me?"

"I love you, Owen, but I do not have time to deal with you right now." She gave the cat a halfhearted stroke as she breezed past and pushed open the door of the diner. She'd make it up to him later.

Kai had to deal with her parents first.

She sent up a few prayers to random gods—the old, forgotten ones, on the off chance that they might have less to do and be free to look after her good fortune.

"Kai!"

Her father greeted her with the same bellow he always did, as if he hadn't seen her in a thousand years, or she'd just come back from some war. Every customer in the diner looked up to see her enter. Sissy Laughlin, who was sitting with her family in the back, smiled and waved politely. Kai waved back.

"Hey, Daddy. Is Mom here? I need to talk to you both."

"Sure, Koukla. She should be here any minute. Come on back."

Normally, Kai would have given her father grief about calling her "doll" like he did when she was a baby, but today she let it slide. Considering the conversation they were about to have, it would be nice to feel like Daddy's Little Girl again for a while.

"Coffee?" he asked Kai as she moved behind the counter.

She nodded. Greek coffee, childhood endearments, and a moment alone with her father would be better than comfort food right now.

"*Dos cafés por favor*, José," he called through the window.

"*Né*," José answered in Greek. Followed by, "Coming right up, boss."

Kai was fairly sure her father knew a few phrases in every tongue on the planet. His enthusiasm for language and life was contagious.

To know Dimitri Xanthopoulos was to love him, and to communicate with him meant having to adopt a unique international language. Kai loved this about her family. It certainly helped on vocabulary tests. And whenever she and her little sister needed to share something in secret code.

Dad unlocked the door to his office and motioned to his guest chair before settling in behind his desk. Kai slid onto the cushioned red leather seat and ran her fingers down the cool rivets along the arm. She'd loved this chair since the time she'd been small enough to curl up on it with her stuffed dog and fall asleep. It felt like home.

Dad leaned back in his huge desk chair and folded his hands over his belly like a Don in a Coppola film. "Tell Baba all about it."

Kai smirked. Her father was an oracle. "Don't you already *know* all about it?" she teased.

"Eh," he shrugged. "I know *something* happened, but the gods can be vague. I'd prefer to hear your side of the story. Indulge me."

"Maybe I should wait for Mom."

They heard the door of the diner bang on its hinges and "WHERE IS MY DAUGHTER?" clearly screeched from the front counter.

"There she is now," said Dad.

Kai could imagine her mother stalking back to Dad's office in a storm cloud, her shoes making a steady clip across the linoleum. The only thing missing was the Wicked Witch theme from *The Wizard of Oz*.

It wouldn't have been far off—Aphrodite Xanthopoulos was an ara, descendent of the Arae, a lineage that gave her an excessively keen knack for cursing people. Though her powers weren't on the mythological level of Circe or Medea, she'd made a close circle of friends in the local coven. Whatever she might have lacked in magic, she certainly made up for in dramatics.

In the next heartbeat, the office door burst open.

"Kalliope!" She put her hands on either side of Kai's head. "Let me look at you. Are you all right?

I cannot believe my own daughter was attacked in this town. The sheriff and I are going to have some serious words." Without so much as a pause for breath, she held up a finger and pointed at her husband. "And *you*! Dimitri Stavros Xanthopoulos, this is all your fault. You gave her a choice to leave instead of making her stay here at the diner where she belongs and look at what's happened! You should be ashamed of yourself."

"But—" Dad began, because letting Kai choose Delaney's had actually been Mom's idea.

But Mom wasn't finished. Her attention shifted back to Kai. "Be honest with me. Did that strange boy hurt you? I can curse his lips so that every bite of food that passes through them tastes like anchovies."

Kai smiled inwardly. Owen would be a huge fan of that one. "Mom, I'm fine. Really, I'm fine. Please. Sit."

She managed to coax her mother down into the chair next to her, but Mom didn't stop talking. "Verity called Roxy, who told Delaney, and then of course Delaney called Pandora when she couldn't find me here. I can't leave this place and spend two seconds with my friends without utter chaos raining down—what, Dimitri? Why are you looking at me like that? Have I confused you somehow?"

"Why would you curse his lips?" Dad asked evenly, as if drawing the question out might slow down his wife's answer. It didn't.

"Because that boy kissed her, of all the fool things. Does he think he's in a movie? Vandalizing local businesses, tearing down busy streets, kissing girls like he's on some sort of last-day-on-earth spree—"

Leave it to Mom to add some perspective. The whole affair sounded much less portentous when she put it like that.

"—I can make sure it's his last day on earth. Was he on drugs? I should have asked Hank to give that boy a drug test. I stopped at the police station first, but Birdie told me Kai had already been and gone but she wouldn't press charges—we'll see about that— and so I headed straight here." Finally, there was a pause for breath. Mom looked Kai up and down from head to toe once more, assuring herself there had been no physical trauma. "Where's your mati?"

Kai's hand instinctively went to her neck again and she remembered that it was bare. From her pocket she pulled the broken silver chain. From it still hung her pale blue, silver-rimmed evil eye charm, now cloudy and cracked on one side from where it had hit the floor.

"Evil eye," or "mati," was the name of both the charm and the curse. An evil eye—the curse— could be given by anyone who meant a person harm...or simply tempted the gods. (Yiayia said that one should not even call a baby beautiful lest the gods decide to make the baby ugly, just for spite.) A holdover from the Mediterranean old world, the mati charm was worn to protect against an evil eye curse, be it given accidentally, or on purpose. As Kai's mother was an ara—a supernatural being who could give curses as easily as she could remove them—Kai and her sister both wore a mati at all times, for their own protection.

"Tsk." Mom took the mati from Kai and threw

it directly in the garbage. "No good anymore. Still, it protected you from something, so it did its job."

Kai wasn't sure how the mati had done anything but fallen off her neck and shattered like any other piece of cheap glass jewelry would have, but if Mom wanted to ascribe mystical meaning to the whole event, well...Kai and her father had learned to just let that go.

But evil eyes protected people from curses, and Aphrodite Xanthopoulos knew curses better than anyone. As strange as this day had been, it wasn't out of the realm of possibility that some of what Mom said might have been true.

"Don't worry. Yiayia brought a bunch of them back from Greece on her last visit, and you know gifts are more powerful than the things you buy yourself. I'll see to it that you have a brand new mati before bedtime."

"Thanks, Mom."

There was a tap on the door—José had arrived with two coffees. Mom took one and handed one to Kai. Kai looked at her father, who just winked in return. Either he hadn't really wanted a coffee, or he had planned on it being for Mom all along.

Kai put her hand around the demitasse cup, savoring a warmth that wasn't coming from inside her for once. She hadn't told her parents about the darkening of the sky, or the Shakespeare, or the fact that she'd known in her bones that he was a wolf. She wasn't sure mentioning any of that would be wise at this point. Or helpful.

She sipped at the rich, thick coffee, sucking down all the bubbles in that first searing gulp. Bubbles on the surface of your coffee meant good fortune, and Kai would happily take all she could get.

Mom sipped at her own cup before asking, "So what are we going to do?"

Dad shrugged. "Kai said she didn't want to press charges, so I think nothing."

"And are we going to let her keep working at that shop so far away from the diner?"

"Mooooooom…"

"Hush. This is between me and your father."

"I would rather have her be happy somewhere else than miserable here, Aphrodite. Wouldn't you?"

Score one for Dad! Mom merely sipped her coffee again and glared at him over the cup. "And Kai, will you be seeing this boy again?"

Well *that* was a weird question. "Why would I?"

"So, he's not your boyfriend?"

Oh. "That's just a story Birdie made up to distract the locals. I promise, I don't even know his name." Kai drank the rest of her coffee quickly down, swirled around the muddy grounds left at the bottom, and placed the cup upside-down on the saucer. She hadn't exactly answered Mom's question about not seeing the wolf again. She had told herself and her friends that there was no sense in seeing him...but that kiss had run through her mind a hundred thousand times since then, and now maybe she wasn't so sure.

The phone in her pocket buzzed. Kai knew it

was probably Bellamy, but she didn't want to check it while the air around her mother still felt so…intense.

Dad shook his head. "This isn't finished. This boy—whatever his name is—I don't think we're finished with him just yet." He picked up Kai's cup, looked inside, and then raised both bushy eyebrows.

"What?"

Dad flipped the cup around so she could see. As usual, the mud had dripped down the side and made columns and patterns. That's where Dad always saw the symbols that spoke to him when reading coffee grounds. But this time, in the very bottom of the cup, the mud had separated into concentric circles. Like a perfect mati.

Mom said a prayer in Greek and crossed herself three times.

Kai's phone vibrated again.

"Huh," Kai grunted. Even with parents like hers, she wasn't sure how much stock she placed on random coffee remains. While her mother was distracted, Kai slipped the phone out of her pocket. There was one text. From Kaley. Kai swiped her thumb across the lock screen.

HIS NAME IS FINN.

4

"Sanctuary" turned out to be a two-story brick house. With shutters. And landscaping. How…quaint. Finn was used to a hay field in the front yard and a cedar forest on the back forty. To be fair, Hank and Ivy's house was conveniently situated at the edge of a patch of dense wood that reminded Finn a little of Tennessee. The good part of Tennessee.

Oh, Tor. You would have loved this, brother. If only they'd come here during their wild tear, instead of that ill-fated trip to Nashville…

Ivy pulled her bike into the attached garage and Finn dismounted as soon as he was able. He resisted the urge to bolt. He had been running for so long—from hate, from family, from fate—it was difficult believing that he'd finally arrived at the place he'd been running to. Trouble was, he still wasn't convinced that he'd be allowed to stay, no matter what Ivy said.

Finn's personal feelings aside, women weren't highly valued in the Kincaid pack. There was little reason to believe Hank Merrow was any different. He'd caved to his wife's demands back at the station, but that might have just been for show. Finn was all too familiar with how abuse played out behind closed doors.

Only…Ivy really *did* look good. She looked healthy. Happy, even. Finn couldn't see a scratch on her, nor had he smelled a whiff of fear. Ivy Kincaid was the smartest, strongest person he'd ever met in his short life. If Hank Merrow had been anything like Harlan Kincaid—or any of his sons—Ivy wouldn't have stayed. And if by some horrible stroke of fate she had, she wouldn't have seemed so…content.

Ivy took her helmet off, shook out her long

hair, and nodded to the rest of the cars in the garage with a grin. "What do you think?"

About the situation? The house? The garage in general? Finn didn't have an opinion one way or another about any of it. What was he supposed to think? What answer would offend her the least? He chose a word generic enough to cover all bases. "Um...great?"

"The word you're looking for is *magnificent*. Or sexy. Our cars are definitely sexy." Ivy raised an eyebrow. "How does a Kincaid escape being a gearhead?"

Ah. Finn understood now. Kincaids were mechanics. Cars were in their blood. Automobiles were their stock in trade, and a measuring stick against which Finn had always fallen short. "Easy," he said. "You screw up enough times, no one wants you anywhere near their 'baby.'"

Ivy laughed. The sound had not changed much over the years, and a small fraction of Finn relaxed. "Well played, cuz. Do me a favor and stay away from our babies too, while you're at it."

"No problem." That was one rule he'd have no trouble obeying. He hoped the rules that were sure to follow were only half so easy.

But Ivy didn't add any rules just then. She walked right into the house, so Finn followed her. Like it was any other day. Like they did this all the time. Like it was no big deal. Finn braced himself for the other shoe to drop, for the yelling to start, for Ivy to turn on him the way the rest of his family had, but there was no sign that any of those things were going to happen.

Ivy flipped through a pile of mail on the table. "So you don't like cars. What's your passion?"

You mean other than Kai? The words were on the tip of Finn's tongue, but he didn't take the bait. "Books."

That stopped her. "Really? I don't remember there being a lot of big readers in the Kincaid family. Or readers of any level. Ever."

"There weren't. Aren't. It's my secret shame." A secret that he'd managed to successfully keep from everyone except Tor. And now Ivy.

"You packed light," she said without looking at him. "You left all your books behind?"

Finn shrugged. "Didn't have any to speak of. Whenever I brought a book home, they got torn up. Or thrown away. A few were burned. I just read whatever the bookmobile has on hand when it comes through." Finn stopped himself. "Or, I did before I left. Classics, mostly. Over and over again. I never have to leave them behind"—he tapped his temple—"because they're all up here."

"Books are a good place to disappear into when one needs to escape."

"Yeah," Finn agreed. Ivy knew perfectly well the sort of hell from which he'd had to escape. She just didn't know the extent. Yet.

Ivy set the mail down and turned to him. "You gonna make me ask? Or will you just tell me already?"

Finn hung his head. Nodded.

"Have a seat," she said.

Finn pulled out a chair and sat.

Ivy waited.

Everything flashed through his mind all at once. Tor. Kai. The pack. The witches. The entirety of his terrible, horrible life since he'd last seen Ivy, all those years ago. "I'm trying to think of where to begin," he said finally. "It's all so messed up."

"Why are you here? Try starting with that."

"I'm so sorry, Ivy. I never would have come if there'd been another choice. You were my last hope."

"I figured," she said. "That's why I'm worried. What I want to know now is just how worried I need to be."

Finn steeled himself. Get the worst part over with first. If she was going to kick him out, better that it happen sooner than later. "I ran from the pack because they think I killed my best friend, Tor."

Ivy went very still. "Did you?"

"*No,*" Finn said adamantly. "It was a bear."

"A bear-shifter?"

"No. Just a plain old black bear."

Ivy squinted. "You expect me to believe a

backwoods Tennessee black bear took out a healthy young wolf-shifter?"

The memory of Tor's death replayed itself inside Finn's mind in perfect detail. Fresh fear and horror swept through him, and he tried not to throw up on Ivy's kitchen table. "It was a fluke," he said. "A lucky strike. Or…unlucky. But not surprising after that witch cursed us in Nashville."

"Okay," said Ivy. "Maybe you should have started with Nashville."

"Tor and I went there a few weeks ago. We weren't supposed to be in the city…we weren't ever supposed to go near heavily populated areas, but the moon was high and Tor got a wild hair and it sounded…"

"Just stupid enough to try?" Ivy filled in.

"Yeah. And we had a blast. Made it all the way downtown to Second Avenue. The lights, the music, the girls in cowboy boots and short shorts…oh, man, Ivy…we…"

"Acted like idiots?" Ivy finished again.

"Pretty much," said Finn.

"So where does the witch come in?"

"Right. So Tor has this theory…" Finn stopped again. He hadn't spoken to anyone since he'd left the pack. He'd gone over the events countless times as he'd run, over and over, but he'd never told the story out loud before. This was the first time he'd had to think of Tor in the past tense. And it hurt. From the inside. The angry fists of the Kincaid pack had left marks and aches, but nothing like this pain.

"Sorry. Tor *had* this theory that if you hit on every girl in the room but ignore the prettiest chick, she's guaranteed to pay attention."

Ivy snorted. "He's not totally wrong."

"I wish he had been. Because the hottest chick at Legends ended up being some teen witch who decided it would be a great idea to curse us both for shooting her down."

"That seems a little extreme," said Ivy.

"She might have been a little tipsy," he said. "Her friends thought it was a laugh riot. Jerks." He'd called them worse things in his head on the run here, but he had no intention of being disrespectful in Ivy's house.

"Mmmhmm," said Ivy. She knew as well as he did just how much trouble supernatural teens had the potential to get into. It was one of the main reasons his pack had always stayed in the woods, kept to themselves.

"Immediately, everything started going wrong," said Finn. "These two randos started a bar fight out of nowhere, but Tor and I were the ones who got thrown out on the street. Then Tor wanted his picture with this guy dressed as a living statue, and while I was taking the photo someone lifted all my cash. It was one bad thing after another—little stuff, all incredibly annoying— until we hightailed it back to the woods and *bam*! Bears." Finn swallowed. "There were no tracks, no sign, no smell. They came out of nowhere, and we had no time to react. One swipe. That's all it took. I ran for my life." A life Tor no longer had, in the blink of an eye. Finn clenched his teeth and bit the inside of his lip until he drew blood. He would not allow any of his weaker emotions to show.

"And then you showed up back home covered in your pack-brother's blood, with no body," Ivy guessed.

"They didn't even stop to ask what happened before they beat me. Not that it would have made a difference. They only stopped because they thought I was dead, too." Finn kept his chin up. "Ivy, I'll understand if you don't want me to stay here with you, or even in Nocturne Falls. But I can't go back to Tennessee. I don't want to put you in danger, and I don't want to cause any trouble with the Georgia pack. If you want me to leave, I'll go. It's okay. All I ask is that you don't tell anyone I was here if they come looking."

"Hey." Ivy cupped his cheek in her hand. "Listen. No Kincaid in his right mind is going to come here for any reason, so don't worry about it. You got that? It's taken care of. *You* are taken care of."

Finn wanted to believe her. "Thank you," he said quietly.

"Now," Ivy said as she rose from the table. "I'm going to make a flourless chocolate cake for dessert tonight, and you're going to tell me all about Kai before my son gets home."

Finn did some quick math in his head. "You and Hank…?"

"Before that," said Ivy. "But he's Hank's all the same. His name is Charlie. You'll love him, I promise." She cocked her head at Finn. "Reminds me a little of you, actually. You know, before this whole bad boy thing you've got going on. Now"— she retrieved a giant brick of baking chocolate from the cupboard—"Kai. Spill."

"I don't even know what happened there," Finn answered honestly.

"Your hormones happened," said Ivy. "I'm just a little puzzled about how it all went down. And why."

"You and me both," said Finn. "I managed to get the sheriff's—Hank's—attention and was tearing down the street, putting on a good show, when all of a sudden there was this voice in my head."

"A voice?" asked Ivy.

Finn scowled and shook his head. "That's not even a good word for it," he said. "It was like someone stuck a needle in my brain and injected words made of liquid gold. Made of her. They felt and smelled and tasted like her. And then when I saw her...I had to go to her. Like the pull of a magnet the size of the moon. I didn't have a choice. And then I was standing right there in front of her, and she smelled like those words smelled, only sweeter—"

"She does work in a pastry shop," Ivy interjected.

"—and I just had to touch her. I had to...taste her."

Ivy fanned herself with the empty chocolate box. "Yeah. *That's* the part we heard about from Verity."

"I don't know what got into me. I've never felt that compelled before, not even during the supermoon. Are you sure she's not a wolf? Not that I've ever felt this way about another wolf— or anyone—but I can't imagine having a connection this strong with someone who's not a wolf-shifter."

"You never know," Ivy shrugged. "She's Greek."

Finn threw up his hands. "Everybody says that like it's supposed to mean something to me. Care to educate your redneck cousin a little?"

"Yes. Sorry." Ivy began melting butter into the bowl with the chocolate. "There are certain countries—Greece, Egypt, Japan, China—where paranormals go so far back in the DNA that almost everyone has some mix of paranormal in their blood. Certain people more than others. For instance, I'm pretty sure Kai's mom is related to Byzantine emperors somehow."

"So how far back are we talking?" asked Finn. "Hundreds of years? Thousands?"

"Back to the gods," said Ivy. "Gods that turned into swans and spiders and trees and flowers...or turned other people into them, depending on their mood. Gods that were born of giants and ate their children. Gods that invented things like fire. And heaven. And hell."

"Got it. So…this chick I met today is a god?"

"On some small level…probably," said Ivy. "Some godlike powers have been known to fade over time. Some, thanks to a few superfluous bards, were never that strong to begin with. But Kai's father is an oracle and her mother is an ara. Which means, whenever Kai comes into her power, however diminished from the beings known as gods, she will no doubt be a force to be reckoned with."

"A force that, for whatever reason, chose me," said Finn. "Great."

Ivy whisked eggs into the chocolate mixture. "Do you honestly think Kai chose what happened between you two today?"

He'd been right there. He'd seen her eyes. There was no faking the shock and fear and surprise and… "No," he said.

"Then we'll call it fate," said Ivy. "For whatever reason, fate made you two cross paths today. That ultimately doesn't have to be a bad thing."

"Except for the part where I essentially attacked

her," said Finn. A case could be made that she'd attacked him first, by pushing her golden words into his head, but he'd been the one to make it physical. He stood up from the table. "I should apologize."

Ivy shoved the mixing bowl into his hands. "What you should do is pour *this* batter into *that* pan, and then get cleaned up before dinner. We've got a lot to discuss when Hank gets home. I don't recommend seeing Kai again until we have a few things settled. And until Hank and I can maybe talk to her parents."

"Right." Finn dutifully scraped the bowl with the spatula as Ivy opened the oven. "Sure. Of course." But his mind was already working on a way to see Kai again.

Golden words and all.

5

This time, he kissed her in the diner. Right in front of her parents and the whole world. Kai couldn't remember if he had started it, or if she had, but it didn't matter. Just like the first time, it was passionate. Thrilling. Magical. Wonderful. Not just perfect, but *correct*. And hot. So incredibly hot.

Who are you? She asked him without words. Her mouth was otherwise engaged, with no desire to stop.

As was his. *Your destiny*, she heard him say without speaking.

But I don't even know who I am yet. I'm not ready for a destiny.

His hands were all over her; everywhere he

touched, her skin burned. *Fate only clears the path. How you walk it is up to you.*

If the choice was hers—if she truly had free will—then she could stop this. She stepped back, breaking off the kiss, fighting every nerve in her body that screamed to be in his arms again.

Kai stared into the wolf's eyes, wondering what to do next. Those irresistible gray irises shimmered gold with desire…and then cracked, shattered like glass and fell to the floor between them.

"No!" Kai screeched.

Finn's words echoed in her head. *My fate cries out.*

Rage fueled the heat in Kai's face and hands and body until she burst into flame.

There was a tap on the window.

Kai's eyes flew open in the mottled darkness of her room. She sat up in bed and touched her cheeks, her arms, her bedsheets, half expecting them all to be covered in soot and ash. But there was nothing. Nothing but slightly elevated heartbeat and the faint colors of a dream now fading like a rainbow.

And three more taps on the window.

She knew it was him even before she pulled back the curtain. Or she'd hoped it was him. Either way there he was on the porch roof, squatting outside her window. He looked like he'd just rolled out of bed himself—he wore dark sweatpants and a t-shirt advertising last year's Nocturne Falls Sheriff's Department Polar Bear Swim Fundraiser. But the boots were the same. The hair, the eyes, the fading bruises, that bottled ferocity…all the same.

Kai crawled into the window seat, unlocked the window, and lifted it. The cool night air swept into her room, welcome on her flushed skin. The breeze smelled faintly of wood and chimney smoke.

He didn't move for the longest time, just sat there, staring at her, saying nothing. Kai settled onto the window seat, hugged her knees to her chest, and did the same. He was beautiful and wild, like lightning. The bruise under his eye seemed to glow beneath the yellow street light, as did several larger ones on his arms. She hadn't noticed them before; he'd been wearing a jacket when he…

Kai felt her cheeks flush again and she broke the silence, if only to distract her one-track mind from its persistent train of thought. "What happened to you?" she whispered.

"My brothers beat me," he said, almost as if it were the sort of thing that happened every day. His voice was a soft growl, like Owen's purr, and she wanted to hear it again.

"How did you find me?"

"I went back to the bakery. Tracked your scent to the diner. Followed your father home from work. Waited until the house went dark."

He had tracked her scent. Well, of course he had, he was a wolf. But hearing it said out loud was still strange. He had come a long way on foot. But then…he'd probably crossed that distance as a wolf, too. And if Dad was home from work *and* asleep, then it really was the middle of the night.

Finn wasn't exactly forthcoming with

information, and though he didn't seem averse to answering her questions, Kai was quickly tiring of this game. "Why?" she said finally. The word encompassed so many questions. She wasn't quite sure which one she was asking, but she hoped he answered anyway.

He looked down at his boots, and her heart mourned the absence of his eyes for that briefest of moments.

Kai seriously had to get a grip on herself.

"I came to apologize," he said. "I won't stay. I just...I'm sorry. I'm sorry that I attacked you today. It never should have happened. I shouldn't have been anywhere near you, never mind forcing myself on you. You're not even a wolf-shifter."

"Were you looking for one?" Kai asked.

"Yeah, actually. My cousin Ivy. Cops brought me straight to her. So that part worked out as planned. But you..."

His eyes met hers again and she melted under the intensity of that stare. She imagined that every woman dreamed of someone staring at her like that someday. Someday. Not now, when she was so ill-equipped to handle it.

"…what *are* you?" he finished.

Your destiny, she almost said, and then stopped herself. "Are you in trouble?"

He shrugged.

"Can I help?"

He shook his head. "I got myself into this mess. I'll get myself out. No sense in dragging anyone else down with me."

Kai picked up on that. "What do you mean, 'anyone else?' Someone who was with you got hurt?"

His brow furrowed; his nod was almost imperceptible. "I won't be the reason you get hurt. I… You…"

Kai knew how he felt. She wanted to say all these incredibly serious things, things far more serious than two people who'd met only a few hours ago had a right to say to each other.

"I don't want to hurt you either." In the back of her mind, those beautiful eyes of his shattered again and the image made her wince. "'My fate cries out,'" she said. "What's that from?"

It was his turn to look startled; the sight was almost refreshing. "*Hamlet*," he answered.

"*Hamlet* again," said Kai. "Why are you always quoting *Hamlet*? Doesn't everyone die in that play? It's depressing."

"Everyone dies in real life," he said. "When did I quote *Hamlet* to you?"

"After you kissed me. 'Proclaim no shame.' I didn't recognize it, but Verity knew. The quote made me think you weren't in the least bit ashamed of kissing me breathless, but now here you are, apologizing. So *are* you ashamed of what happened?"

He opened his mouth as if ready to defend himself, but before he spoke he narrowed his eyes at her. "You said *always* quoting."

"In my dream just now," she admitted. "You said the line about fate." She saw his mouth twitch slightly and his lip curled...was he laughing at her? "What, you think it's funny that you're in my head?"

"You were in mine first," he growled. "On the street. I heard you tell me to keep running. I heard you tell me not to hurt your friends. But wolf-shifters don't talk to each other like that, not with perfectly-formed words that echo like a loudspeaker in your brain. So I'll ask again...what are you?"

"I don't know," she said, exasperated. He seemed annoyed by her answer, so she tried to explain. "Really, I don't know anything more about myself. My parents both came into their powers at thirteen, but my thirteenth birthday came and went without so much as a glimmer. This is the first evidence I've heard that I have any abilities at all. The question is: why you? Why were you the one that heard me on the loudspeaker?" She sat up, tucking her knees under her. "Do we mean something to each other? Could we?"

He leaned toward her, close enough that she could almost feel the heat of his skin. "I don't see how," he said. "Wolves don't mate outside their species and you're not a wolf, despite"—he waved his hand back and forth in the small gap between them—"whatever this is."

Kai didn't know what to call it either, but the compulsion was strong. She wanted to fly out the window and leap into his arms and have her way with him right there on the roof of her parents' porch and that was *not* Kai. Kai was the kind of girl who did her homework on the table at the diner and never stayed out after curfew. She had never been like this. Sure, she'd had the odd crush on boys at school here and there, or in movies, but never…whatever this was.

No fantasy she'd ever had about a movie star had even come close to the intensity of that dream.

"Besides," he said. "You have a boyfriend. Even if you were a wolf, I had no right to kiss you."

Kai's half-gasp came out as a choke. "I'm sorry. What? What boyfriend? Was Birdie telling more of her stories? If you heard that information over the loudspeaker, then you were definitely kissing the wrong girl."

His nostrils flared. "I can smell his stink all over you even now. Cats love to mark their territory."

Could he be talking about Owen? Owen had never been in her house...that Kai knew of. There was nothing to say that he couldn't have tracked her from the diner just like the wolf had. But Owen was just a cat. Everyone knew that humans didn't date cats. Were wolf-shifters really that possessive?

Kai shook her head. "No. No way. I mean, there's this stray that hangs out at the diner and follows me around sometimes and gives me grief, but that's it. I wouldn't even call him a pet." A friend, yes. A best friend, even. But definitely not a pet.

He backed away from her. Only slightly, but enough. Kai forced her body not to fall out the window after him. Wolf hormones and magic-induced whatever aside, he was just a boy. A strange boy. A strange, beautiful boy that had taken up residence in her head and quoted Shakespeare in her dreams. Kai was reminded of another tragic play about two teenagers who had fallen for each other through an open window. That hadn't ended well for anyone involved either.

"Whatever," he said. "Either someone is lying to you, or you're lying to yourself." He ran a hand through his hair. Kai's fingers wished they could do the same. She clenched them into fists. "I have no reason to lie to you. I have no reason to be here at all."

"Then why did you come?" said Kai.

"To apologize."

"Well, you've done that. So why haven't you left?"

In a flash, his hand was behind her head and he was kissing her again, as slowly and deeply and passionately as he had in the dream. Only this definitely wasn't a dream and therefore infinitely better. Kai's blood sang. Her heart threatened to explode in her chest. If they'd both tumbled off the roof right at that moment, Kai was sure she could have flown them both to safety on wings made of pure joy.

Stay. She thought the word with all her might until it echoed inside her mind. Maybe if they kept talking, kept trying to figure this out, they could find an answer. *Please. Stay with me.*

I can't, she heard him say, without having actually spoken.

Her gasp ended the kiss. She tried to read the expression in his furrowed brow. The wind caressed a dampness on her cheek, and she wondered if they had been her tears, or his.

"Finn," she said as she reached for him, the first time his name had crossed her lips.

He backed away, out of reach, as if it was the hardest thing he'd ever had to do in his life. "Goodbye, Kai," he said. And with a leap, he disappeared into the darkness.

Kai would not say goodbye. Could not. She put a hand over her heart and pretended it wasn't breaking. Why? Why did this strange wolf have such an effect on her? What was this magical connection? This horrible, aching feeling...was this what falling in love was like? Kai certainly hoped not. Because if it was, she had no intention of ever doing it again.

She shivered and moved to close the window. Just as she'd turned the latch, she heard a small clatter on the sill. The necklace her mother had given her that evening had slipped from her throat, broken just like the one before it. Kai picked up the mati and examined it…sure enough, despite the incredibly short distance it had fallen, the eye had shattered.

She still had a million questions where Finn was concerned, but right then, Kai was absolutely certain about two things.

One: However it happened, Finn was one seriously cursed wolf.

Two: Owen would get that follow-up on his verbal sparring match with Kai…but he wasn't going to like it.

6

"Finn? You have a visitor."

Finn took a deep breath, pulling himself out of the black hole of sleep. He pulled a book out from between his head and the pillow and blinked as his eyes focused on his strange surroundings. Bookshelves. Baseball bat. LEGOs. Video games. He experienced a brief moment of panic before he remembered Ivy ordering him off the couch and into Charlie's bed right before she took her son to school.

Finn had stayed out most of the night. He'd gone for a run after his meeting with Kai and the kiss that never should have happened...*again*. He still felt safer in the woods than he did in a building, safer as a wolf than as a man. Wolves slept and ate and ran and followed the moon where it took them. Men had to deal with hearts and lives and families and politics.

Last night's dinner had been dominated by politics—a discussion mostly between Ivy and Hank. Finn felt it wise to continue keeping his mouth shut. Charlie, who really was as good a kid as Ivy had said, watched them all with big eyes, but stayed as silent as Finn. Finn wondered how much Charlie really knew about his Kincaid relatives. Based on his expressions that night, Charlie was learning a lot. Finn just hoped his little cousin never had to gain that sort of knowledge firsthand.

Since the Kincaid pack thought Finn was dead, Ivy and Hank made the decision to not disabuse them of that notion. Hank Merrow might have taken a Kincaid to his bed, but once the marriage was done and the alliance sworn to, he and Ivy had had no contact with the rest of the Tennessee clan. Even if they had suspected Finn was still alive, there was no reason for any of his old pack to seek him out in Georgia. That was good news. The less he had to worry about his pack hunting him down and ending him, the more he could worry about getting out from under this curse before it killed him…or anyone else he got close to.

Ivy knocked on the door again. "Finn, sweetie? Are you awake?"

Finn grunted a growl and realized he was still in wolf form. He shifted so that he could answer his cousin. "Yeah. Up. I'll be down in a sec."

Groggily, he forced himself into a sitting position on the side of the bed and stared at his toes. After all he'd been through, one short night wasn't nearly enough. He needed about a week's worth of sleep. And a shower. He wondered if his mysterious visitor was willing to wait that long.

And then he remembered that he only knew one person in this town besides his family.

Finn leapt to his feet and reached for the door, stopping only because he caught a glimpse of himself in the mirror hanging on the back of it. His clothes were rumpled, his hair was wild, and the fading bruises on his face made him look like a serial killer. He needed to fix what he could. And quick.

He slipped out of Charlie's room and into the bathroom where—thank the moon—Ivy had left a pile of fresh clothes and bathroom supplies for him. In record speed, he splashed water on his face and brushed his hair and teeth. He changed into jeans and a long-sleeved shirt, to cover what bruises he could. He skipped the shoes. When he was finished he sped out of the bathroom, grabbed either side of the staircase railing, and made it to the first floor in one flying leap.

But the person waiting for him in the entranceway was not Kai. It was a tiny blonde girl with rainbow streaks, enormous wings, and a cheerleading uniform. The top and skirt were black, edged with deep, blood red. On her chest, above her crossed arms, the word "Harmswood" was stitched in what looked like silver glitter.

Finn had no idea who this girl was. But the look on her face said that she had one serious bone to pick with him.

"I have iced tea, if you kids want to sit out on the back porch," Ivy called from the kitchen.

"Thank you, Miss Ivy," the fairy drawled. She brushed past Finn, heedless of the wings that almost took out his good eye. "Come on," she said to him impatiently.

"Bellamy, are you already out of school for the day?" Ivy asked as she filled the tall glasses.

"No, ma'am. I have a free period right now while the squad goes over our routine for the Scaresgiving Parade. It's pretty much a variation on what we did for Panic, so it's not particularly important for me to be there."

"This town does love their parades, don't they?" said Ivy. "And Bellamy, you don't have to call me ma'am."

"I was raised in South Carolina," Bellamy explained. "Tryin' to take 'yes ma'am' and 'yes sir' out of my vocabulary is like askin' a sailor not to cuss."

"Fair enough," Ivy laughed. "I'll be out in the garage changing the oil on my bike. If you two need me for anything, just holler."

Bellamy sipped her tea and strolled onto the back porch as if she lived there. Finn followed her, curiosity outweighing his thirst.

"Your ears aren't pointed," he said.

"Well aren't you the Rhodes Scholar." She set her tea down on the table. "I am not 'fae' like you know them here. Where my family comes from, fey blood runs in a multitude of races: fairies, piskies, sprites, the green children, the blood court…even some humans. And not all of us have pointed ears."

"Yeah, but you look like something that flew straight off the page of a Disney coloring book."

Bellamy cocked her head. "And you look like the rejected pretty boy from a sparklin' vampire novel." She held up a hand at his snarl. "But that's not why I'm here, is it?"

Finn wondered how much force it would take to snap that tiny little neck between his teeth, and just how much trouble he'd be in with Ivy if he did so. "Why are you here? Who are you?"

"I am Bellamy Merriweather Larousse," she said.

"Your girlfriend's best friend."

Finn snorted. "Kai is *not* my girlfriend."

"No she's not, and thank you for verifyin'. That cockamamie story Miss Birdie told earlier did rather sound like a load of bull, and I know my girl like I know my back handspring, but in this town, it's always good to double-check." She crossed her arms over her chest again. "Especially after that steamroller of a kiss."

He shouldn't have—he knew he shouldn't have—but her body language practically begged him to goad her. Finn raised an eyebrow and gave Bellamy his most devious smirk. "Kiss? Which one?"

"Oh...*you*!" Bellamy exclaimed. She tapped the bracelet on her left wrist with the palm of her right hand and then flicked her fingers at him in exasperation.

The world around Finn suddenly grew larger— the trees, the house, the fairy, everything. No, he was growing *smaller*. He finally stopped shrinking, but it took a few extra moments for the sky to stop spinning. He fought the urge to vomit and realized that he couldn't move his neck. He reached a hand up to his forehead…only to realize that he had no hand. What had been his arm was now dark brown, segmented, and covered in bristles.

"What have you done?!?" he roared, but the words came out like he'd swallowed a balloon full of helium.

Bellamy crouched down. If it hadn't been for her black bloomers, he'd have been able to see straight up her skirt. "I came here to have it out with you, Finn Kincaid, and I refuse to be distracted by your devastatin' handsomeness. I swear, all you wolf boys are so alike, it's pathetic."

Finn would like to see her say that to Hank's face. "What did you do to me?"

"Don't worry. It's just a bit of fairy dust. Should last long enough for us to have a decent conversation."

"Am I a butterfly?" he asked, without really wanting to know the answer.

"I turned you into a cockroach," she said. "Far more appropriate." She scooped him up and placed him gently on the table, then plopped herself down beside him with all the flourish of a princess. "There. See? That's much better. Now we can talk eye to eye, like civilized people."

"You're a civilized nutcase," said Finn.

"Don't make me squash you," warned Bellamy.

"Look," said Finn. "There's no need for all this. I went to see Kai last night."

"To attack her again with your lusty wolf lips?"

"To *apologize*." Finn found it incredibly difficult to stress the gravity of one's words when one was a talking bug.

"Well, now. Gold star for that. Anythin' else you'd like to share?"

Finn's patience had shrunk proportionately with his size, and he hadn't had much to begin with. "If you really are Kai's best friend, wouldn't she have told you the sordid details of our meeting already?"

"She wasn't in school today," the fairy said. "And unlike *some* people, I respected my friend's trauma enough to give her some space."

Finn recognized the undying loyalty. He and Tor had had that same loyalty for each other, once upon a time. Finn wondered if anyone would ever feel that way about him again. "Kai can have all the space she wants," he said. "I had no intention of being in her life before yesterday, and I have no intention of being in it now. I can't hurt her if I'm not around, can I?"

Bellamy shook her head. "You kiss the stuffin' out of my best friend—more than once, I take it—and then inform her that you have no intention of followin' through with anything. Oh, yes, I'm sure she's just peachy. Not hurt in the slightest."

When Bellamy put it like that, it made him feel as small as he currently was. "I can't undo what's been done, and I'm sorry for that," he said. "But taking myself out of the equation was the only way to make sure no harm would come to her."

"Why? Because you're a dangerous scary werewolf who can't control himself?"

"Because I'm cursed."

Bellamy pinned him with those huge, kaleidoscope

eyes. "You mean, curse-cursed? Or 'havin' a super-bad day' cursed?"

"I mean my pack-brother and I caught the wrong end of a witch. Tor's already dead. The rest of my pack beat me to within an inch of my life because they were convinced I killed him. It's only a matter of time before I shuffle off this mortal coil myself."

The fairy covered her gaping mouth with her fingers. "Oh, my stars."

"I don't suppose fairy dust can do anything?" Finn asked.

"Goodness no," said Bellamy. "Fairy dust is fair-weather magic that shifts with the wind and fades with the dawn. It's as flighty as I am. Affects big time spells about as much as a fly affects a windshield. A witch's curse…that's big time." Bellamy sucked her teeth. "Bless your heart. And here I come along, threatenin' to enchant you more than you already are."

"If I didn't have this black cloud over my head, I promise I'd be quaking in my boots."

Bellamy actually laughed at that. The sound

tinkled like silver bells over water. "You're very kind to say so."

"I don't suppose you know a way I can get rid of this?" he asked her.

Bellamy's laughter died. "I hardly know you. You blew into this town like a hot tornado, and I'd love nothin' more than to see you blow right out again. Why on earth would I ever want to help you?"

"You wouldn't," he said. "But you know Ivy and Hank and Charlie. I can stay away from Kai, but I can't stay far enough away from them while I'm staying here. And I suspect you want to hurt them about as much as I do."

Bellamy smirked. "You got me there."

"So? Do you know any witches?"

"Darlin', this is Nocturne Falls. You can't throw a stick without hittin' a witch."

Finn tried to be more specific. "Do you know one that can help me?"

Bellamy's brow furrowed. "Now, that's a horse of a different color. Most of the witches here all belong to the local coven. If you get one involved, you get them all involved. They don't take cursin' lightly. I suspect there would be an investigation, interrogation, the whole nine yards. You want to go that far?"

"Maybe," Finn said. If he could handle this whole thing himself, Ivy would have to be proud of him. Maybe even proud enough to let him stay. "Is there a way to start small?"

"Hmm." Bellamy pursed her lips. "Unfortunately, the most powerful witches at Harmswood are also the most popular girls in school."

"So…that would be 'witch' spelled with a 'b?' Sounds a little like the one Tor and I met."

"You don't know the half of it."

"I thought cheerleaders were always the most popular girls in school. Wouldn't that make *you* the most popular?"

"You watch too much television, Mr. Cockroach. At Harmswood, power means everythin'. Power and money."

"Okay then, do you know any slightly less powerful witches?"

"Well, there's Kaley—she's a whiz at reading auras, but she's still quite young. And her father's girlfriend is really active in the coven, so that would be tough to keep a secret. Oh!" Bellamy snapped her fingers. "*Duh.* Maya! Of course. I'm an idiot for not thinkin' of her first."

Finn wanted so badly to remark on Bellamy's general capacity for idiocy, but he considered their relative sizes and reconsidered the snarky comment. "And this Maya, she can hold her own outside the coven?"

"I believe she can. She's got a lot more power than she's willin' to admit, even to herself. She's not from Nocturne Falls originally—her family's from Central America."

"Central America?"

"Guatemala, specifically," said Bellamy. "She was raised bruja. Serious, old school magic. Is that a road you're willin' to go down?"

"Do I have a choice?"

"Point taken," said Bellamy. "But I'll have to ask her first. I don't want you forcin' another one of my friends into doing somethin' against her will."

Finn bared his teeth at the fairy and growled from the pit of his belly.

It came out as a squeak.

Bellamy laughed so hard that tears came to her eyes. "I'll swing by after school and pick you up, tough guy. That is, if it's all right with Maya." With that, she lifted her glass of iced tea off the table and made her way back into the kitchen. "I've got to get goin', Miss Ivy, but thanks for the tea," he heard her call to the garage. For such a tiny thing, that fairy sure had a set of pipes. "And I turned Finn into a cockroach, but he'll be fine. Toodles!"

Wait, she was just going to leave him here like this? He heard the front door slam. Yes, apparently she was. Finn peeked over the side of the table. Even knowing he could survive it, it looked really far down. With his luck—his curse—he wasn't willing to chance it. He'd just have to wait here until Ivy showed up or he changed back, whichever came first. He hoped it would be the latter.

It wasn't.

"Well, well." His cousin wiped her hands on a rag. "Fairy cut you down to size, didn't she?" Ivy the Giant bent down and grinned over Finn like the Cheshire Cat. Man, she had a lot of teeth. "Good girl," she chuckled.

"She said it wasn't permanent."

"It's not," said Ivy. "Enjoy it while it lasts."

Finn growled again. "This town is certifiable!"

Ivy pulled a chair up and sat across from Finn. "This town has its own way of doing things, which you'll learn, in time."

Finn couldn't imagine. He'd only ever lived around wolves, who settled their arguments with fists and teeth. Having so many different kinds of paranormals in a small town like this was chaos. With all this power floating around, how did it not just dissolve into anarchy? Figuring out Nocturne Falls might take forever. Finn didn't know how much time he had left...but Ivy did seem willing to give him some.

"So I can stay?" As soon as Finn asked the

question, his form shifted back to that of a very large teenager. The table beneath him collapsed.

Ivy reached out a hand to help him up. "The jury's still out, but you can stay for now. In the meantime"—she sighed at the remnants of the little table—"go take a nice long shower and make yourself presentable. I'll fix you something to eat."

"Yes, ma'am," he said as he headed for the kitchen, half because he'd been Bellamied, and half because he knew it would irk her.

"Hey Finn?"

He turned back to his cousin. "Yeah?"

She smiled again and nodded at the table. "I'm glad you're making friends."

7

The best thing about having workaholic parents was that they both understood the value of a mental health day. Kai worked hard in her classes and didn't abuse her excused absences, so when she told her parents that she needed a day off from school after yesterday's hullaballoo, they gave it to her without much grief.

The second best thing was that workaholic parents were usually *at work*. And with Mel at school, Kai had the house to herself the whole morning. A nice, quiet house in which she could finally think about...everything.

For a few hours, she simply sat in her bed and stared at the window. She couldn't stop replaying her meetings with Finn, one kiss after another, over and over. She wasn't entirely sure she wanted the memories to stop. As complicated as the whole situation was, there was something to be said about being irresistibly desired by such a force of nature.

He'd sworn he'd stay out of her life, but Kai didn't believe that for a second. Take away the tourists, and Nocturne Falls was an incredibly small town. The only way Finn would be able to avoid her completely would be to leave. Since Ivy had been his destination—his sanctuary—Kai guessed that Finn wouldn't be going anywhere soon. Nor would her problems.

Somehow, she needed to get past the kissing.

She closed her eyes, hugged her pillow and remembered one more time what it was like to be so unabashedly *wanted*. Then, with a sigh, she stood up and got dressed. Before she saw Finn again, she had another shifter to deal with. She was not looking forward to this conversation. She wasn't ready to lose one of her best friends. Especially at a time like this.

But if Owen really was what Finn said, how would she ever be able to trust him again?

Kai poured herself a bowl of cereal and wondered how best to confront the cat. The time was now. The place… well, she could bike up to the diner easily enough, but the conversation they needed to have wasn't something she wanted to do in public.

And then she remembered what Finn had said about cats marking their territory. She was making this far more complicated than it needed to be. Kai let the spoon drop back into the bowl with a clatter and walked out onto the front porch.

"Owen, I need to talk to you."

Kai didn't scream the words, but said them loud enough so that any cat hiding in the general vicinity would be able to hear her. She didn't have to wait long.

"Ready for another round? This time, if I win, I demand a bowl of cream and a fresh can of tuna. And not that chunk-light nonsense. I want the good stuff." The pixie cat casually stalked up the front steps and Kai looked at him with new eyes.

Verity was right: he was scrawny and scruffy, but still far too well-groomed. A true stray animal probably wouldn't have thought to take such good care of himself. Even one who could talk to Kai.

"We are far past tuna," said Kai. "Come inside."

"Okay." Owen wound a casual loop in and around her feet before darting through the front door and tearing up the stairs.

"Owen!" Kai called after him. He was not making this easy. Then again, when had he ever? She followed him up the stairs and found him curled up on her window seat, tail lazily flipping back and forth.

"Score one for the cat," Owen purred. "I always wanted to see your room. It's nice. Suits you."

"Thanks." Kai needed Owen to stick around for the rest of this talk and not run away again. She considered standing in the doorway to block the exit, and then decided shutting the door altogether would be the best solution.

"Uh-oh. Am I in trouble?" he crooned.

"Sort of, yeah."

"And…did your family get a dog? I didn't think you had a dog. What is that I smell?"

"Enough!" Kai marched over to the window seat and made sure the curtain was fully closed. She didn't want anyone—local or tourist, human or supernatural—witnessing this exchange. "I have had it with you animals and your territories. This is *my* territory, do you hear me? *My* bedroom. *My* life."

"I understand," said Owen. "Despite my misgivings about your recent career choice, I am one hundred percent Team Kalliope."

"Is that so?" Kai felt her eyes begin to water and she forced herself to keep her emotions in check. She'd known Finn less than twenty-four hours, and yes, his leaving made her ache…but not like this. She and Owen had been friends for years. After all the times she'd poured her heart out to him about the big stuff, the little stuff and everything in between, he'd never breathed a word about being more than just a cat. His betrayal felt like a knife to the gut. "If you're really on my team, Owen, then you will stop lying to me. Right now."

"I'm sure I have no idea what you're talking about."

"Yes," Kai said with as much calm as she could muster. "Yes, you do. Go on, shift."

Owen hissed his displeasure and hopped down from the window seat. Suddenly, a young man stood before her. A tall, thin, very disoriented young man. Kai stepped forward as if to help him, but Owen caught Kai's bed post with one hand and held the other up in a signal for her to keep her distance.

"Score one for the baker," he said. His voice was the same but different, deeper now that it came from a human-sized body.

Kai stared at Owen as he composed himself. It was difficult to wrap her mind around the fact that this was Owen the cat, Owen the pain in the neck, Owen her best friend... and yet, it wasn't.

He was beautiful in the way that all shifters are beautiful, lean and lithe and muscular. It was an easy enough thing to tell—his clothes hung off his frame in tatters. He was tawny from head to toe, golden brown hair and skin, and eyes, she assumed, though he hadn't looked at her yet. If Finn was the moon, all shadows and darkness, Owen was the sun. His fingers were long and slender, his wide eyes were slightly tilted, and there was a sprinkle of freckles across his nose. But no whiskers, no tail, no fur. She'd half expected his ears to be as pointed as they had been in cat form.

Kai closed her eyes and shook her head.

"What's the matter? Don't like what you see?"

That was absolutely not the case, and Owen's beautifully annoying self knew it. "Part of me really wants to punch you right now. A lot."

"I'm not sure what's left of my clothes would hold up to the sort of tousle you have in mind."

Kai bit her tongue to avoid laughing. Point to Owen. Maybe two points, because she opened her eyes to look at him again, which was undoubtedly what he wanted. It was so strange—so wrong— seeing him this way. If she'd passed by this young man on the street, she never would have known it was the same cat she talked to for hours every day. And yet…his eyes. His eyes, though larger in size, were that same, familiar pale green and gold.

"Why didn't you just tell me?" Kai asked.

"It was meant to be a secret," he said.

It was hard for Kai not to feel insulted. "You seriously thought I wouldn't keep your secret?"

"It was meant to be a secret *from you*," he clarified.

"Why?"

Owen attempted to start three sentences before finally settling on, "It's complicated. But that doesn't make me any less sorry for having to keep this from you. I'm so, so sorry, Kai."

He sounded a lot like the wolf at her window last night. "Everyone's apologizing to me today," she said. "I'd rather they not have a reason to in the first place."

"You're right, of course."

"What happened to your clothes? I thought shifters kept all their clothes when they changed shape."

"We do, but I've been a cat for a hundred years now, or more." He looked down at what remained of his shirt and trousers. "And there wasn't much to them when I shifted the first time."

"A hundred years? Are you serious?" Suddenly, without warning, her inner Greek hostess kicked in. "Can I get you some food? Water? New clothes? I'm sure Dad has something that would fit you. Sit down, at least, before you fall down."

That part he did, at least, easing back on the window seat in relief. "My darling Kai," he said. "Always thinking of others before yourself."

Even in a different body, she recognized that tone of voice, and she was not about to give him the upper hand. "Don't go buttering me up just to change the subject, Owen. I know what you're like." Kai stopped herself. "But I don't know. Do I?"

"Not all of it," he said. "But you do know me. That part is real, Kai. Our friendship is real."

"I want to believe that," she said honestly. "I

want to give you the benefit of the doubt."

"Thank you."

"Granted, this"—she gestured at his new form from head to toe—"gives me great cause for doubt."

"I know," he said. "But no matter what secrets I've been forced to keep, I promise I never would have hurt you. You know that, don't you?"

That one thing Kai did believe. "Yes."

"Not everyone would be so understanding. You're really a remarkable person. I hope you know that."

Kai might have believed every word he said, if it hadn't been for that feline condescension she knew so well. "Save the compliments until after you've explained what the hell is going on. But first, let's get you properly dressed and fed, okay? As much as I want to hate you right now, you're still my best friend until I decide otherwise. And I can't talk to you with you looking like that."

Owen raised an eyebrow. "Like what? Half naked? I don't mind if you don't."

Kai threw up her hands.

"Point for the cat." He smiled at her, and she almost lost her resolve to be angry with him. "You know you love me."

"Yeah, I do. Jerk. For now, anyway. Come on, I'll start the shower for you and you can get cleaned up while I find you some decent clothes."

He sang in the shower. She hadn't expected that. Not that she was familiar with any of the old tunes, but—unlike Finn—the sound of Owen's voice put her at ease. It was easy enough to find an extra pair of black slacks and a Mummy's Diner polo in her father's dresser; it was his standard work uniform. She grabbed a belt, too. Owen might not stay so lean after he had a month of decent meals inside him, but in his current state those pants would fall right off him otherwise. And Kai already had enough distractions of the gorgeous male shifter variety.

She opened the door of the refrigerator and wondered how to feed a shifter that hadn't eaten human food for a century...or even decent cat food, for that matter. Nothing too heavy or complicated, for now. She knew that shifters liked meat and carbohydrates, so she settled on cold cuts piled on a giant fresh hoagie roll, no frills.

"You know, I'd heard about long, hot showers before. If I had any idea just how decadent they were, I might have come out of hiding a long time ago." Owen padded down the steps in his bare feet, still toweling his short hair dry. He caught sight of the sandwich just as Kai was cutting it in half. "You are a goddess." He tossed the towel onto the counter, sat on the bar stool beside her, and dove in.

"Easy now," she said. "Go slow. I don't want you barfing that up in my shoes later."

The look he gave her as he chewed was pure ice.

Point for Kai.

"What?" she said innocently. "Isn't that what cats do?"

Owen swallowed. "I'm devastated that you think I'd behave like such a plebeian."

"Says the man who just wolfed down half a

sandwich the size of my head." It was odd using the word "wolf" anymore. As soon as she said it, Kai wished she hadn't.

If Owen noticed, he made no indication. "And I'm about to disappear the other half. Want to time me?"

Kai waited until he'd taken a huge bite to test her theory. *Can you hear me?* she thought to him while his mouth was full.

Of course I can, darling, Owen answered without missing a beat. *Always could do.*

Always? Since when?

Since we met. He took another bite. *Since you were thirteen and started coming into your powers.*

Wait…do you know what I am? What I'm going to become?

Owen shrugged. *Not completely sure, but I have an inkling.* He gave her a lusty wink and she punched him playfully on the shoulder. *Decided to give me that trouncing after all?*

Considering it. She added out loud, "You still owe me an explanation."

"Right then." Owen shoved the last bite of sandwich in his mouth and made quick work of it. "I'm not your typical shifter, of course. Was human, through and through, before that blasted Sphinx."

"You were cursed by a Sphinx?"

"Mmm…I don't know that 'curse' is the right word to use when dealing with certain ancient entities. There's a legend that says if you stare into the Sphinx's eyes long enough, you could turn into a cat."

"I've never heard of such a thing," said Kai.

"Doesn't mean it's not true. After all…" He waved a hand around himself with a flourish and then groaned. "Are sandwiches supposed to make you tired and a little sick?"

Kai gave a half laugh. "They are when you eat them as fast as you just did. Come on, you'll be more comfortable on the couch. Just don't lie down. I don't know if this was common knowledge a hundred years ago, but it's not a good idea for humans to lie down after eating."

She took his hand and led him into the living

room. He plopped down on the couch with a sigh and pulled her down to sit beside him.

"So what on earth made you stare into the Sphinx's eyes long enough to be transformed?" Kai had to ask.

Owen closed his eyes and leaned back on the pillows. "A beautiful woman. Incredibly, breathtakingly beautiful." He peeked at Kai. "Almost as beautiful as you." She slapped him again on the arm, but this time he caught her fingers and kissed them. "I have missed being human," he said contentedly.

"So why didn't you just change back before this?"

"The short version is, I wasn't sure I could. Or what would happen if I did. The rest is a very long story not worth telling at the moment."

Kai doubted that. She snatched her hand out of his affectionate clutches. "Owen, I still don't understand. Is this...telepathic communication my power?"

"One of them. I suspect there will be more. It's

why I was sent to find you."

"You were…" Kai could tell from the evenness of his breath that he was in danger of falling asleep on her, so she pinched him.

"Ow!"

"You were sent to find me? By whom?"

"By terrible people, and the less said about them, the better. They bade me find you so that I could ask you to do something when your powers fully manifested. As they have yet to do so, it's a moot point. In the meantime, you and I get to enjoy our lives. And sandwiches." He yawned. "And naps."

Kai shouldn't have been surprised. Owen hadn't acted much differently when he was a cat. Fill his belly and stick him in a ray of sunshine and he was as good as dead to the world. She needed to say something compelling enough to keep his attention.

"I'm guessing this new power of mine is also behind the interminable compulsion I have to hook up with a wolf-shifter? It would explain a few things."

That did the trick. Owen sat up, fully awake and alert. "You want to do *what* with a wolf-shifter?"

"Oh, don't get me started," she said with exaggerated dreaminess. "He came by the bakery sometime after you left yesterday. He stopped by the house last night, too. Kissed me both times and then told me he didn't want to have anything to do with me…but I have to say, I don't quite believe that. Call me crazy, but I think we're destined to be together."

Kai took a small amount of pleasure in Owen's bewilderment. He shook his head as the words began to sink in. "That dirty dog," he said. "That's what I smelled in your room. Or should I say, *he*."

"My head has been so messed up. I wanted to talk to you about it, or Bellamy…there just hasn't been time. And then last night, Finn said that he had no right to kiss a girl that was already taken. He meant I'd been taken by *you*. But of course, I couldn't have known that."

"Oh, Kai." Owen took her hands in his. "I truly

am sorry. You believe me, don't you?"

Reluctantly, Kai nodded. There were still a lot of things Owen hadn't told her—a hundred years' worth of things. She suspected she was still missing quite a bit of vital information. But she was willing to give him time to catch her up.

Unlike Finn, who had just walked away.

"So do you love him?" Owen asked at the look on her face.

"I don't even know him."

"That's not an answer," said Owen. "And I should know. I'm a cat. I can obfuscate with the best of them."

Kai debated whether or not to open up to him. But they couldn't salvage what friendship they had left if she started holding back now. "Can I tell you something that will sound strange?"

"Always."

"It feels like my body's in love with him, but my mind hasn't caught up yet. Does that make sense?"

"It does," Owen nodded. He put his arm

around Kai and pulled her against him; she rested her head in the curve of his shoulder like it was the most natural place in the world to be. Lazily, he stroked her hair as she relaxed into him.

"Are you purring?" she asked after a while.

"Sorry, habit. Does it bother you?"

"No, it's just...odd. Kind of comforting, actually. I'm more familiar with that side of you."

"I am too," he said.

They sat there for a long time, quietly, in the sunshine. But Kai couldn't stop her mind from racing. She'd thought Owen was asleep when his voice interrupted her busy brain.

Are you thinking about him? The wolf?

Yes, she answered.

But he doesn't matter anymore, right? Since he's taken himself out of the picture?

I didn't ask him to, Kai answered. *I would have given him a chance to explain himself, to get to know me. A chance just like I'm giving you. Everyone deserves a chance.*

But I already know you, said Owen. *You are too*

good a person, my darling Kai. You are aware that wolves only mate with their own kind, and they leave a trail of broken hearts along the wayside until they do. It's only a matter of time before he hurts you.

He said he didn't want to hurt me, said Kai. *And I believe him. Like I believe you.*

Owen planted a brotherly kiss on her forehead. *I will still stand beside you, no matter what happens. When Finn leaves for good, I will still be here for you. I will protect you.*

It did Kai's heart good to hear that, but she suspected that Finn might say the same thing about Owen. There were still too many unanswered questions. Why had he been sent to find her? And how? What sort of supernatural did he think she was? Why had he lied about his nature for so long? What was Owen going to ask her for when she came into her full powers, assuming they were even what he thought they would be? If bad people had tricked him into becoming a cat and forced him to spend a hundred years hunting her down, it more than likely wasn't anything small. Or good.

It couldn't have been a coincidence that Finn and Owen had both popped into her life right here, right now. Kai couldn't shake the feeling that a storm was brewing, and that she was smack in the center of it.

She really, really needed to talk to Bellamy.

8

"I am not getting in that thing."

After a ridiculously long and blissfully hot shower, Finn was clean for the first time in ages. Even his leather jacket and boots were free of the Tennessee dirt and clay. Ivy had made sure that he was well-rested and well-fed. Apart from a few lingering aches beneath the worst bruises, he finally felt like the respectable badass he was: a young wolf-shifter, powerful and dangerous, destined to be adored and feared.

There was no way he was riding shotgun in a pumpkin.

Bellamy took her foot off the gas and coasted into the driveway, turning so that Finn could witness the rolling of her eyes full force. "My brother works as a tour guide here in the Falls. Since I have had a very long day on my feet, he was kind enough to lend us his ride for the evenin'."

Her brother's "ride," best that Finn could tell, had once been a golf cart. It had been outfitted with a bright orange domed ceiling, crafted to look like a jack o'lantern that had happily eaten its riders. Finn gave the—cart o'lantern?—another once over and raised an eyebrow.

Bellamy folded her hands over her chest. The cheerleading uniform had been replaced by a shimmery pink sundress that picked up the iridescence in her wings and completely clashed with the rest of the vehicle. "Do *you* have a car?" she asked.

Finn shrugged. "No license." Even if he'd had a car out in the woods, it's not like there was ever anywhere to go that he couldn't get to in a quick wolf-run.

"Then unless you're going to pay for a cab or carriage to come pick us up—both of which look remarkably similar to this in the Falls—I suggest you get over your ego and step in."

Reluctantly, he obeyed. "I could run. Can't you fly?"

"There's a spell on the water in this town that keeps the humans from askin' questions about our natures," she explained. "We try not to push that more than we need to. All set?"

"As set as I'm going to be," Finn said as Bellamy made a quick three-point turn and scooted back up the driveway. "I'm not used to being this conspicuous."

Bellamy flashed him a wicked smile before flipping a switch on the dashboard. The entire mouth of the pumpkin lit up with orange and green twinkle lights. The Vincent Price prologue to Michael Jackson's "Thriller" began echoing prophetically from a speaker hidden somewhere in the dome.

Finn winced. He shook his hair into his face and slouched as far down into the seat as he could go. Darkness couldn't fall across the land fast enough.

Bellamy, on the other hand, seemed to be enjoying herself more than a princess on a parade float. With the wind in her colorful curls, she sat tall and greeted everyone she knew as they whizzed along. Which was literally *everyone*.

"Do this very often?" Finn mumbled.

"I've taken the wheel from time to time," she said. "We like to have a cart or two handy in case one of our dancers or gymnasts takes a spill."

The comment confused Finn. "Considering the dazzling array of superpowers your squad no doubt possesses, I can't imagine that happens much."

Bellamy punctuated her next princess wave with a neighborly toot-toot of the pumpkin's horn. "We have accidents more than you might think. Our goal as a squad is to execute each and every exhibition with no magic at all, since we perform for the public so often."

Finn found the thought of a winged fairy with a sprained ankle rather humorous. "And then what, the jack o'ambulance takes you to the witch doctor?"

She turned her sternest expression on him. "A doctor that uses magic is called a Healer. A witch doctor is something completely different, but I suspect you already know that. Don't be insensitive. This town is already predisposed not to like you."

"I've noticed." He would have to have been blind to miss the scowls directed at him by every person they'd passed. "Are you required to say hello to everyone in town?" As if the pumpkin itself didn't draw enough attention.

"Yes, I am," said Bellamy. "Because I want you to get a sense of just how many people in this town will chew you into tiny little pieces if you mess with Kalliope Xanthopoulos. Hello, Miss Frances!" she called over the pumpkin's soundtrack.

"Good afternoon, Bellamy!" Miss Frances called back. "Ready for the parade this weekend?"

"Takin' one last test run," Bellamy answered.

"Sounds good. You be careful now!" Finn felt sure Miss Frances had directed that last part at him.

"Yes, ma'am," Bellamy said, and then turned

down the next side street.

Finn was impressed by the house whose driveway they turned into—he wasn't sure he'd ever seen so much green in his life, and he'd grown up *in the woods*. This house was more like a jungle, thick with leaves and flowers lining every path, in front of every window, and hung from every rafter. There was a curvy young girl filling some of the flowerpots on the front steps; she stood at their arrival and put her hands on her hips.

"Seriously, Bellamy? If I hear 'Monster Mash' one more time, I'm going to throw up on your pom-poms."

With a sigh, Bellamy turned off the lights and music.

"*Thank* you." Finn extracted himself from the cart, banging his head on the pumpkin as he did so.

"I wasn't talking to you, hot stuff."

Finn reined the charm back in and stopped short. Like Bellamy, this young witch had a way about her that was warm and hostile all at the same time. Finn was used to hostility; the Kincaids breathed, slept, and ate hostility for breakfast. It was the graciousness that threw him off. Plus, he knew these young women were only circling the wagons for Kai. Once they realized that he truly had no intention of harming her—or seeing her ever again…

"Whatcha plantin' there, Maya?" asked Bellamy.

Maya brushed her soiled hands against her cutoff jeans—unlike most gardeners of Finn's acquaintance, she didn't wear gloves. He admired a woman who wasn't afraid of a little earth. "The usual fall stuff," she said. "Simon and Garfunkel, cilantro and chives. Hey, Cursed One, grab the rest of that bag of potting soil and follow me around back, willya?" With that, she picked up her trowel and disappeared into the thick greenery.

"What's 'Simon and Garfunkel?'" Finn asked the fairy.

"Parsley, sage, rosemary, and thyme," answered Bellamy. "You know, like the song. Come on, now.

Maya doesn't like guests who dawdle."

Finn suspected Bellamy was making that up, but he followed along anyway. After only about three steps, the swirling sound of a magic wand erupted out of nowhere. Finn froze, his hackles raised. The last thing he needed right now was to be ambushed by another spell.

"Calm down, it's just my phone." Bellamy pulled a giant cell phone out of a tiny pocket in her skirt that hadn't been there before and checked the screen. "Oh, sugar," she cursed.

"Do you need to be somewhere?" asked Finn. "Top of a pyramid? Or a float?"

Bellamy narrowed her eyes at him before putting the phone back in her magical pocket. "Nothin' you need to worry your pretty little head about."

If Finn had thought the front of the house impressive, the backyard—with its enormous semi-detached greenhouse—was phenomenal. Maya led them inside. She tossed her trowel in a bucket and showed Finn where to place the bag of soil. Then she led them to a sitting area in the back of the greenhouse where the walls sprouted orchids and violets. There was a round stone table with a few items on it: a mirror, a cigar, and a bottle of rum.

"My mother won't be home for another couple of hours, so we have time to screw this up." Maya lifted a white candle and metal wand. Finn braced himself to witness some magic...until he realized the wand was just an elongated lighter. "At which point, if we've screwed things up *too* badly, she can step in and fix it." She looked at Finn. "Hopefully."

Bellamy sat down on one of the three stone benches that circled the table. "What spell did you decide to use?" Finn had considered asking the same question, but he didn't particularly care as long as his curse got lifted.

Maya lit two more white candles and placed them on the table. "I did some curse research online during my last study period, and then followed it up with some deep digging through Mom's private library when we got home. The subject matter, ingredients and warnings…let's just say things got dark and complicated really quickly. But then it occurred to me: we need to start small. Super small. I mean, we don't even know what we're dealing with. Right?"

Finn realized that she was talking to him now. "Yes. Right. The witch's curse was aimed directly at Tor, but it encompassed the both of us."

"You don't happen to remember what the witch who cursed you said, do you? The exact words?"

"Not all of it. It happened so fast." Finn glanced at Bellamy. "And what I do remember I wouldn't repeat in polite company."

"A wolf with manners. Heaven forfend." Maya sighed and lit another candle. "Come whisper it in my ear."

Finn did.

"Yeah, that's bad enough," Maya agreed.

"Bad enough for Tor to die first," said Finn.

"This is why magic users don't curse out loud,

if they can help it," said Bellamy. "There's just too much at stake to be casually tossin' off stuff like that."

"Did you hear what I told Maya?" Finn asked her.

Bellamy waved a hand. "No need. I can guess."

The swooshing wand sounded again from Bellamy's magic pocket, followed by a bird chirping from the back of Maya's shorts.

"Is Kai texting you too?" Maya asked the fairy.

"Yes," said Bellamy. "There's somethin' she wants to show us, or tell us... I feel horrible. Like we're betrayin' her by tryin' to help him." Bellamy said "him" as if Finn were something she'd scraped off the bottom of her shoe.

"So tell her." Finn preferred to keep his attempt at getting rid of this curse on the down-low, but he didn't see any reason they should lie to Kai and endanger their friendship. "I said I'd stay away from Kai, but I didn't force her to make the same promise. If she wants to come here, that's entirely up to her. I promise to keep my hands to myself."

"It's not your hands I'm worried about, darlin'," said Bellamy.

Maya chuckled.

Finn held said hands up in defeat. "I'll promise whatever you want as long as Maya can still help me with this spell." Inside, his stomach was doing flips. He wanted Kai to be there almost as much as he wanted this blasted curse lifted. But focusing on his predicament would be a lot easier if Kai wasn't around distracting him with her...self.

"Would you be okay with Kai coming over?" Bellamy asked Maya. "It is your house."

Maya shrugged. "Fine with me. Go answer her while I finish setting up. Make sure she knows what she's walking into." Bellamy nodded and wandered back into the depths of the greenhouse, tapping on her phone. Maya lit another candle and placed it on the edge of the table. "You've brought chaos into our world, wolf."

Finn tried to be charming without seeming devious. For all that Ivy teased him about making friends, it would make living in this town easier.

Even if they were Kai's friends too. "You're welcome to call me Finn," he said. "And sometimes a little chaos can be a good thing."

"Yes, it can." Maya started to smile, as if remembering something, and then caught herself. The smile turned into a grimace. "But chaos only works in our favor when everything else goes right." She set another wick aflame. "So we have to work extra hard to make sure everything goes right."

"Is that why you're lighting all these candles?"

"White candles are for purity and protection," she explained to Finn. "I'm going to have to light a black candle for this spell, and I'm not a huge fan of black candles."

Finn knew as much about witchcraft as he did about cars. "What's so ominous about black candles?"

"Asks the Man in Black himself?" Maya teased. She began lifting the lids of jars and collecting dried leaves into her hand, pinch by pinch. "Like any witchcraft, power can be used for good or evil. The bias lies in the intention of the witch. But certain things tap into bigger powers, older powers, powers closer to the veil of death or the edge of chaos. Black candles can be used to summon powers like that. And I don't know what Bellamy's said about me but I'll be the first one to tell you, I'm just not that good a witch."

"'There is nothing either good or bad, but thinking makes it so,'" Finn quoted. He looked into her eyes, their depths as dark and rich as the soil she'd just been planting in. "For what its worth, I believe in you."

"Thank you," said Maya. "But if belief was everything, horses would fly."

"Are you sure they don't?" asked Finn. "I'm beginning to think anything is possible in this town."

"Perhaps they do." Maya grinned, and then caught herself again.

"Why do you keep doing that?" Finn asked. "The frowning thing?"

Maya concentrated on the herbs in her hands.

"Because I don't want to like you. And you're making that very difficult."

Finn started to answer that, but Bellamy skipped back into view, her multicolored curls hopping about drunkenly. "Kai wants us to wait for her."

"That's fine," said Maya. "Gives me time to set more protections. Can't hurt, and I need the practice anyway. Why don't you go out front and keep an eye out?" She waited until Bellamy skipped away again before turning back to Finn. "Bellamy would never ask, because she honestly thinks we live in the best of all possible worlds, but…are you okay with this?"

"Okay with this spell about to be performed by an unpracticed witch? With a curse hanging over my head that might kill me and everyone I care about at any moment? With the one girl I can't seem to resist in this town popping over to witness my incredible failure at life firsthand? No. I am not okay." Finn bowed his head. "No offense, of course."

"None taken," she said. "It's refreshing to hear such honesty from a wolf."

Whether or not she revealed it willingly Finn did not know, but suddenly all the pieces fell into place. Some time, at some point in Maya's past, a wolf had done her wrong. Finn felt compelled to apologize on behalf of his species, though he wasn't quite sure why. "If I could take this curse and give it to the wolf who betrayed you, I would."

Maya's eyes widened briefly in surprise, and then she sighed and smiled. "I—unlike some witches—am not a fan of putting bad things out into the universe, no matter how richly it is deserved. But that thought counts. Thank you."

Finn liked this witch. She was earthy where Bellamy was flighty, tough without being hard. He could see what might have drawn a wolf to her. And now that he'd said his piece, he felt it was now up to him to lighten the mood. "Or, I'm lying through my teeth because at the end of this charade I plan on eating you all for dinner."

Maya laughed a little as she ground the dried herbs into powder between her palms and sprinkled them over the stone. "But you're not lying," she said as the savory scent filled the air. "That's the one gift I have that I'm absolutely sure about. I can always tell if someone is lying."

9

As fast as Kai biked to Maya's house, her tires should have been smoking. As soon as Bellamy had called to say that she and Maya were helping Finn with his curse, a fire had started in Kai's belly. She was mad at her friends, but grateful for them; mad at Finn, too, but excited to see him again; and still mad at Owen, just for good measure. She used the fire of her anger to fuel her as she pedaled through town, faster and faster.

Bellamy was waiting for her on Maya's front stoop, a fairy in her natural habitat: surrounded by leaves and flowers. Bellamy pulled her phone out of her magic pocket and checked the time. Twice. "That was fast."

Kai hopped off the bike and swiped the kickstand down. "I was strangely motivated."

"I'll say so. What's so important that it got you here like greased lightnin'?"

"Where's Maya? I want to tell you both together."

Bellamy stuck her thumb out over her shoulder. "She's in the greenhouse with the wolf."

"That's fine."

"Is it?" Bellamy scrutinized her. "Is it really?"

"Yeah," said Kai. "Finn already knows. Sort of. Come on." She took her best friend's hand and dragged her down the path that led to the greenhouse.

"This ought to be interestin'," Bellamy said in her wake.

Maya and Finn were at the back of the greenhouse, seated around a table full of candles and talking like they'd been friends for years. Finn had his back to them, but Maya looked...happy. On any other day, Kai might have been jealous over the intimate setting. *Let her have the wolf*, Kai thought. *One less problem for me to deal with.*

Finn froze mid-sentence. He stood up and walked to the far side of the table before turning to face her and Bellamy. "Kai," he said by way of greeting.

Oh, crap. "You heard that, didn't you?"

His eyes spoke volumes, but all he said was, "Yes."

"Sorry." Lesson number one, after she figured out if this telepathy worked with anyone besides Finn and Owen, would be learning to put the kibosh on her wayward thoughts.

"Heard what?" asked Bellamy.

"You got me," said Maya. "But I'm intrigued."

"Apparently, I have the ability to communicate without words," Kai explained.

"You're talking about telepathy," said Maya.

Kai nodded. "It's why Finn stopped running in the street that day."

"Because he heard you say that you wanted him to kiss your face off?" asked Bellamy.

"No." Finn's voice was a growl. "She didn't

want me to hurt her friends." He addressed Kai without actually looking at her. "I didn't think you knew I could hear you."

"I didn't, at the time. Owen helped me figure it out this morning."

"Owen the cat?" asked Maya.

"Cat-shifter," Finn clarified.

"*Cat-shifter?*" Bellamy almost screeched.

"I didn't know either," said Kai. "Finn helped me figure out that one."

"How much you want to bet if I hadn't, he'd still be playing cat?" asked Finn.

"Well *that's* super creepy," said Maya.

"He's been in cat form for a hundred years or so," explained Kai. "The Sphinx put him under a spell. It's a long story." *Most of which I haven't heard yet*, thought Kai. *But I don't need to worry them about that right now.*

And then she caught Finn looking at her, this time with an eyebrow raised.

Did you hear that too? she asked him.

Yes. His voice in her head was like warm honey

dripped down her bones.

Sorry. I'm trying to get better.

"Okay, stop that right now," said Bellamy. "It's rude to have a conversation in front of other people that they can't hear."

"She's right. And yet all my Central American relatives do it anyway," said Maya. "So...wait. Are you telling me there's some hot Egyptian guy at your house right now?"

"He's British," said Kai. "But, yeah."

Maya put her head in her hands. "Chica, I don't know what part of your power suddenly developed into shifter catnip, but you best be spreading some of that around."

"You know as much as I do now," said Kai. "It's been a fairly exhausting couple of days. Whoa...has it even been more than twenty-four hours?" The realization made her a little dizzy.

"You poor thing." Bellamy patted her back. "Maybe you should sit down."

"No, I want to try this telepathy thing first. On you and Maya. I want to see if I can make it work with people other than Finn and Owen, and if not, then I want to figure out why not."

"Okay. Fire away." Bellamy balled her fists and slammed her eyes shut.

"Bell," said Maya. "She's not going to shoot you in the face with a Super Soaker. Relax."

Kai concentrated, focusing all of her energy on Maya and Bellamy. *CAN YOU HEAR ME?*

Finn winced.

"Oh!" Bellamy's eyes popped open. "I did! It was like gettin' a phone call while drivin' through a tunnel."

"Or from a can connected by a string," said Maya.

"Hooray!" Kai clapped her hands. "I can practice... getting better reception. I just wanted to know if it was possible. And it is! The rest we can work out later. I am starting to get a bit of a headache." She also didn't want to continue blasting Finn's mental eardrums with her thoughts. It was curious that Finn and Owen could hear her so easily. "Besides, we have a curse to vanquish, right?"

Maya looked over her table of protection. "Your mother is the Curse Queen, Kai. She should be doing this, not me. Heck, after we perform this scrying spell, I might still recommend that we ask her."

"Noted," said Kai, just as Finn said, "I'd rather not."

Maya held her hands up to stop both of them. "One thing at a time. First, we figure out what's going on. *Then* we worry about how to proceed."

"So you're gonna scry something?" asked Bellamy.

"In addition to having prophetic qualities, a scrying mirror also has the ability to show the truth of things when one looks into it," said Maya. "With my particular gift, you can imagine what a failure I've been at trying to see into the future."

"But you can use the mirror to amplify your truth gift?" asked Kai. "Cool."

"I'm about to light a black candle," said Maya. "If we come out on the other side of this without summoning a demon from hell, *then* you can tell me it's cool."

Bellamy, Kai, and Finn stepped as far back from the table as they could while Maya prepared. She poured a shot of the rum and used a pair of gardening shears to cut the end off the cigar. She lit the cigar with the elongated lighter, and then lit the black candle in the center of the table. She took a few short puffs on the cigar, gagged, and took a few more puffs, until a thick white cloud hung over the table. She drank the shot of rum—gagged again—and then took another puff off the cigar. This time, she blew the smoke onto the mirror.

The surface of the mirror turned black.

The spell was working.

Bellamy took Kai's hand and squeezed it.

"Come," Maya said to Finn. Her voice sounded deeper, her irises now as black as the mirror. Finn stepped forward and took the mirror in his hands.

From over his shoulder, Kai could see his reflection. There was an aura around him that seemed...sick. Broken. Green like a fading bruise and cracking with gold lightning. For a moment her nostrils filled with the scent of licorice.

"What is that?" Finn asked Maya.

"That is the curse," she answered.

"Can you remove it?"

"I don't know," said Maya. "It's oddly simple. Deceptively simple. I'll have to consult the books, but from what I'm seeing here, it just looks like bad juju."

"That's it?" spat Finn. "That's ridiculous! This thing killed Tor. How could something as simple as bad juju be responsible for killing my pack-brother?"

"Which is exactly why I'm suspicious." Maya put a hand on Finn's shoulder. "Even still, something as simple as a skipped beat can stop a heart."

"Fine. So if it's that simple, you can just take it off me, right?"

"Maybe," said Maya. "It's just...all of your fabulous faith in me aside, I'd be more comfortable calling Kai's mom in on this one. It could be nothing. Or, it could be ten times more complicated than it looks and I'm totally unprepared for it, and your body starts falling apart, piece by piece to make food for the demons."

Finn bowed his head. Kai knew why he didn't want to ask for help. He had vowed to stay away from her, to keep her from harm, and petitioning her mother to remove his curse would go against all of that. She suspected it had been hard enough for him to seek help from her friends, but Kai knew firsthand how difficult it was saying no to Bellamy Larousse.

Maya stamped out the cigar, but its thick smoke still hung above the table. "If I ever perform that spell again, it's going to be with cherry soda and bubbles. Or cough syrup and a smoke machine. Because that was disgusting."

Bellamy did not pick up on Maya's attempt at changing the subject. "I say we go to Kai's mom."

"There is no 'we,'" Finn growled. "You have no say in this."

"You don't want my help any more, fuzzbutt, then fine. You won't get it." Bellamy spun on her heel and stomped back through the greenhouse.

Kai looked to Maya, who shrugged. Kai was the only one capable of diffusing this situation. She took a deep breath and turned to Finn, bracing herself for rejection all the while. "Look, I know you said you didn't want to be around me or whatever, but really, it's fine. Maya's right. My mom knows curses backward and forward. I'm sure she could get rid of that thing without you losing any of your major body parts." Finn didn't move, nor did he make any response, so Kai risked coming a little closer. "Bellamy has a good heart. When she sees a problem, she will do all she can to fix it. She cares about what happens to you, whether she wants to or not. We all do." Kai looked to Maya, who nodded. Boldly, Kai took another step closer to him, close enough to see her reflection in the mirror.

At first, Kai did not recognize herself. Her olive skin was dark now, almost purply-black. Her wild curls were now a mass of snakes writhing about her face. Her irises had turned completely gold. Animal's eyes. Wolf eyes. At her gasp, a pair of giant wings unfurled from her back. The feathers were not white, like in fairy tales, but silver gray. Like a wolf's fur. On the hand that came to her black-lipped mouth, the fingernails were made of flame.

If she had been the one holding the mirror, she would have dropped it. Instead, Finn simply set it on the table, reflection-side down. She knew that he had seen the monster inside her true self. That horrifying chimera.

"I don't want to see your mother," he said without turning to look at her. "I don't want anything to do with you." Instead of walking off, as Bellamy had, he shifted into a black wolf before them and sped away.

Kai couldn't speak. She couldn't breathe. She felt tears in her eyes, but she wasn't crying. Maya quickly thanked the spirits and blew out all the candles on the table, black first. She forced Kai to sit while she cracked open a window and coaxed the cigar smoke out of it.

"Did you see that?" Kai whispered when she found her breath. "Did you see…me?"

"I did," said Maya.

"And it didn't freak you out?" asked Kai.

"Surprise me? Yes. Freak me out? No." Maya took a seat beside her. "Both of our families come from some serious old world magic. We'd be naive to think that there wasn't some weird godstuff lurking in our DNA."

"Are you sure we were looking in the same mirror? Because I didn't see a god. I saw Medusa. Or a close relative."

"Kai," Maya breathed. "Your eyes are brown, with a little green, and a dark circle around the irises. Know how I know that? Because I have looked in your eyes without turning to stone. You are not Medusa."

"Then what am I?" Kai asked desperately. "I counted at least three animal aspects—wolf eyes, wings, and let's not forget that awesome snake hair—I could also have goat hooves and a scorpion tail for all we know."

Maya shrugged. "Manticores with scorpion tails were always cooler in my opinion."

"*Maya*."

"What? They are. Sue me. You know, all those animal bits are probably why you have such an easy time communicating with Finn and Owen."

Maya's deduction made perfect sense, but Kai didn't really want to talk about Finn right now. "You're not helping."

"Fine. You want help? Let's suss it out. But first...I have to move this. Because it stinks and it's making me sick to my stomach." Maya picked up the tray where she'd stamped out the cigar and promptly dumped the contents into a watering can. She slid the tray onto a workbench and dusted off her hands. "Right then. So from what I know about Greek mythology—"

"You know about Greek mythology?"

"Only because of you. What we learned in school only scratched the surface. When you first told me your mom was an ara, I wanted to find out more. So I did."

"How very scholarly of you."

"Hush now," said Maya. "The scholar is talking.

There are actually many women in Greek myths with snake hair and wings. Did you know? Probably because men were scared of their wives…"

"…and rightfully so," finished Kai.

"Did you also know that the gorgons were originally protectors of the oracle? Your Dad's an oracle. You being a gorgon is not out of the realm of possibility. Personally, I think you're more like your mother."

"Just what every girl wants to hear." Kai thought about the fire she'd been feeling lately—in her belly, in her cheeks, in her whole body—whenever she was upset…or passionate…about something. And then there had been the literal flames at her fingertips. "Even at her most upset, I have never seen my mother's hair turn to snakes."

"I highly doubt yours will either, outside a magic truth mirror," said Maya. "But an ara is related to the Furies. If you ask me, I think that what we just saw reflected in that mirror was the natural state of a Fury."

Kai thought back to old stories she and her sister had heard at the table during family gatherings. "That's not a bad guess, actually. My great-great grandmother was a Fury," she said. "Plus or minus a great, maybe. I can't remember exactly. She was also a late bloomer."

"That could be important," said Maya. "What else do you know about her?"

"She came into her power during the Great Fire of Smyrna, back in the 20s." Kai did some quick math—the genocide had happened almost a century ago. Almost as long as Owen had been a cat. Kai put her cool palms on her now-hot cheeks. Having witnessed the fire she possessed literally at her fingertips, her constant blushing and overheating made so much more sense now. "They burned her house and killed her husband. She rose from the flames, cursing her attackers while guiding her children to safety. At least, that's how the story goes. Furies are especially vengeful when children are the wronged party."

"That's some serious power, Kai. And

honestly…I don't know that I'd trust anyone but you with that kind of power."

"But I'm a *monster*."

"Come on, Kai. I know you. You are a good person, inside and out."

Owen had said much the same thing about her. "I'm not nearly as good a person as Bellamy."

"No one is as good as our bleeding-heart fairy," said Maya. "But that's not the point. If you turned full-on scary Fury tomorrow"—she gestured to the upside down mirror—"which I'm positive that you won't, you would still be a good person who does good things. In my book, that doesn't make you a monster." She played with the dried herbs on the table, drawing swirl patters with her finger. "'There is nothing either good or bad, but thinking makes it so.'"

Kai blinked. "Did you just quote *Hamlet?*"

"Finn did," said Maya. "I was telling him earlier how bias lies in the intention of the witch, and it seemed appropriate. It applies here too, I think. Furies have great and terrible power, yes.

Vengeance, retribution, anger, hate, Darth Vader and the whole nine yards. But if I recall, they have the power to be benevolent too. Like most gods. So…be benevolent."

Kai wasn't sure what to think or how to feel in this moment, but she did know one thing: she had the best friends in the world. She leaned over and hugged Maya tightly. "I think I need to have a little talk with my parents."

"Good luck with that," said Maya. "If you need me for anything, just let me know." And then, in a very Maya-like way, she answered the question Kai hadn't asked. "Finn will come around eventually. Give him time."

"I don't know about that," said Kai.

"I had a chance to talk with him a bit while Bellamy was outside waiting for you. I'm not saying we're best buds or anything, but he strikes me as a pretty decent guy. For all his bad boy facade, Finn's a little country-come-to-town—"

"The Falls is not for the faint of heart," Kai interjected.

"—but like you, he's dealing with a lot of stuff right now. Don't freak out about the mirror, okay? Talk to your mom first. Go easy on yourself. And...go easy on Finn. Give him a chance."

"Please. He doesn't want a chance. You heard him. He doesn't want to have anything to do with me. Right?"

Maya put her hands on her hips. "Chica, if you need my skills to tell you that was a bold-face lie, you're dumber than I thought."

10

"Finn, your ride's here!"

Finn heard Ivy call out to him from the backyard and he came running. He bounded out of the woods and made a flying leap onto the back patio, shifting from wolf to human by the time his boots touched the ground.

"What ride?" he asked, dreading another outing in Bellamy's musical jack o'lantern.

"Kai's mom is here to pick you up. I'm sure I mentioned it."

Finn was sure she hadn't, because he almost certainly would have had something to say about it. All of which he managed to convey to his cousin now, without saying a word.

Ivy stood her ground. "Look, I know that you've got this thing about needing space from all of us because you're worried you're going to kill us all with that curse of yours, and I respect that. Heck, I even admire it. But we've given you a couple of days to cool off, and that curse isn't going away on its own."

"I told Kai I didn't want to have anything to do with her," Finn huffed. "I'm sticking to that." Ivy didn't need to know all the particulars...like the second kiss, or the scrying spell, or the slight chance that he might actually be making friends in the Falls. Friends that, between them, were capable of harnessing an incredible amount of raw power.

His annoyingly tall cousin reached out and tousled his hair before he could duck away. In Ivy's eyes, Finn would always be that little boy hiding under the bed. "It's sweet how you kids think you have a say in these things. We have the means to deal with curses in this town, so we do. Simple as that. Aphrodite Xanthopoulos is the best, bar none. You'd be a fool to turn away that kind of help. So you won't." She tossed him his jacket. "She and I have discussed your situation at great length. Now she's waiting for you in the driveway."

As much as he hated to admit it, Ivy was right. This curse of his was like a bad virus. He was covered in fresh scrapes and bruises from random evil branches and clumsy stumbles. A wolf-shifter only ever looked like that if he was ill, totally inept, or exceptionally unlucky. And his cousins were not immune. Just yesterday, Ivy had broken her favorite pie plate. Charlie had come home with a failing grade on what should have been a simple math quiz. And something was going on at the police station that Hank hadn't discussed with the family, but it was bad enough to have him fuming over dinner last night.

Finn had tried holing up in the woods and staying away from the house, but the grass and trees around his warren were starting to die faster than the autumn world around them. He had to get rid of this curse. And if the best person to do that was the mother of the girl who tugged at his heart, plagued his dreams, and made him crazy…well, that just sounded like part of the curse, too.

Aphrodite Xanthopoulos looked a lot like her daughter only older, of course. Her hair consisted of the same wild brown curls, only shorter and more well-tamed. There was a permanent furrow in her brow and what he suspected was a similarly-permanent fire in her eyes. Finn didn't need any more clues to tell he was in the presence of a matriarch, so he attempted to behave accordingly: by keeping his mouth shut.

Kai's mother examined him for an uncomfortably long time after he got in the car. Finn got the sense that she was sizing up his curse as well as his overall person in general. Finally, those fierce eyes left him and she turned the key in the ignition. "It's a good thing you've stayed away," she said. "But now it's time to be done with this thing that plagues you."

"Yes, ma'am," he muttered.

"Call me Mrs. X," she said as she backed out of the driveway. "All the kids do."

"Thank you," he said as she shifted gears, meaning so much more than gratitude for the familiar name. This wasn't the way he wanted to do it, but by the end of this day his curse would be gone. After so much loss, there was a light at the end of the tunnel.

Somehow, be it supernaturally or just from motherly intuition, she sensed all of that. "You are destined to be in our lives for a long time, Finn Kincaid. Ivy says you're a good boy." She looked back at him with those eyes of fire. "Do your best to stay that way." And then she put her foot on the accelerator and started down the street. They made it all the way out of the neighborhood before spotting the first set of police lights.

"Oh, bother. I thought we'd beat the parade route setup. Hold on, we're taking a detour." She pulled into a driveway beside the flashing barricade and turned the car around.

Finn had forgotten about the parade. Bellamy had mentioned it on her first visit in uniform, and then again in regards to that ridiculous pumpkinmobile, but he hadn't given it a second thought at the time. However, knowing that the bothersomely saccharine fairy would be otherwise engaged while he underwent this curse removal made Finn almost happy. With any luck, Kai would be out on the street cheering for her best friend, and he wouldn't have to subject himself to further humiliation.

A cursed wolf has no such luck. Maya and Kai were both waiting on the steps as they pulled in.

"No desire to watch the parade?" Finn asked them.

Maya snorted. "You already know my feelings on 'Monster Mash.' Besides, there's one of these like every other month in the Falls. I need another Halloween parade like I need another hole in the head."

Kai's answer was significantly less jaded. "Mel and Kaley went," she informed her mother. "I told her that was okay, and to call you or check in with Dad at the diner if she wasn't home before dark."

"That's fine," said Mrs. X. "Those two have

been inseparable lately."

"Who's Mel?" Finn asked Maya.

"Melpomene," Maya said. "Kai's little sister. Mrs. X didn't want her around for this. You know, in case we turn your insides out or blow up the house or something."

Finn felt sure Maya was joking, but the young witch's face remained completely unchanged.

"Come on in," Mrs. X called from the top of the stairs, and they all followed her through the front door. The house smelled like humans and central heating and recently baked bread...and cat, but only faintly. Kai's duplicitous little friend was hiding somewhere. If the cat had any brains at all, he'd stay hidden.

"Can I get you anything to drink? We have water or tea in here, and there are sodas out in the garage. And are you hungry? I brought some appetizers home from the diner. Or I could warm up some tiropitas in the freezer. Wouldn't take but a minute."

"Stand down, Mom. Finn came here for his

curse. Not lunch." Kai rolled her eyes. "Greek hostesses always have the dial turned to eleven."

"I could eat," said Finn. He was a wolf. He could always eat.

Maya elbowed him in the side. "You might want to stuff your face *after* we do the big spell."

"Right." Finn thought back to Maya's comment about the possibility of him being turned inside out. "Maybe later."

"Suit yourself," Mrs. X said as she shut the fridge. She moved to the cabinet, removed a mug, and poured herself a cup of coffee. Maya and Kai took two of the three barstools at the counter and invited Finn to take the last.

So they were doing this here? In the kitchen? Finn was fine with that, he just guessed the spell would be performed in some windowless basement with walls covered in pentagrams and ancient runes and things.

He still had a lot to learn about this town.

"Curses…" Mrs. X stopped, took a sip of her coffee, and began again. "No, that's too complicated. Let me start somewhere else. Maya told me about using the scrying mirror, so let's talk about mirrors. Did you know that breaking a mirror is not really seven years' bad luck?"

"It's not?" asked Finn.

"Not unless the mirror was already cursed to begin with. However, the simple act of saying 'If you break that mirror, you'll have seven years' bad luck' is all you need to curse it."

"You mean, if a magical person says it," said Finn.

Mrs. X grinned and saluted him with her coffee cup. "Everyone has magic, young man. Just some more than others. This is why we must always watch what we say, good or bad. Because even when we are not watching, you can be sure that fate is."

"And gods love nothing more than to be meddlesome," said Kai. "Just like parents."

"What can I say? I'm a meddler extraordinaire. If anyone steps on a LEGO in this town, it was probably my doing, and they undoubtedly deserved it." Mrs. X reached across the counter and pinched her daughter's cheek. "All kidding aside, I'm sure the girls have told you that the supernatural folks in this town do not take curses lightly. If a witch here is caught misusing magic, she is banned from magic completely for five years."

"And if she does it again after five years, what happens then?" asked Finn.

"They kill her," Maya said flatly.

Mrs. X clucked at the girl's answer. "No, no…but the matter is brought up to the coven to discuss a steeper fine. Could be banishment. Or being stripped of powers altogether. Or both." She took another sip of her coffee. "Now, back in the Ottoman Empire, they'd just find the source of the problem and melt her face off. After she was drawn and quartered, of course."

Maya grinned like the cat that ate the canary.

Speaking of cat…Finn unobtrusively sniffed the kitchen. That stray shifter of Kai's had been here— in this house—and recently. Was he still here? Maybe…up in her bedroom? Finn sniffed again. He wondered what went on between them. He doubted a cat would be chivalrous enough to keep his distance while Kai dealt with her troubles.

The thought that he remained one of Kai's troubles gave Finn a strange thrill.

Mrs. X was snapping at him. "Pay attention. This is important."

"Yes ma'am," said Finn. "Sorry."

"The curse you have is something we call 'the Bad Penny.' Simple enough and easy to remove"—Finn perked up—"but, it never truly leaves you. You will have to come back here every so often and have me remove it again."

"Forever?" He tried not to look at Kai as he asked the question. So much for his plan to stay away. This was not the answer Finn had hoped for.

"Forever," said Mrs. X. "Unless we can find the witch who cursed you and ask her to remove it herself."

"Or kill her," Maya added.

Kai narrowed her eyes at her friend. "You are in quite the morbid mood today."

"It's the parade," said Maya. "Makes me extra stabby."

"You're almost frightening enough to have your own float," Mrs. X said to Maya. "Because you're not entirely wrong. A witch's death usually ends her curse. Obviously, taking that direct route is frowned upon."

"Obviously," Kai said pointedly.

Maya stuck out her tongue.

"Which is why I asked Maya to help me out with this," said Mrs. X.

Maya pulled her tongue back in and did her best to look mature.

"I want to try the scrying truth-mirror again, but on a slightly larger scale."

"Another black candle?" Finn asked Maya.

"Unfortunately," she said. "But no more cigars. Hallelujah for that. The rum was bad enough, but that cigar made me sick."

"We've evolved beyond a lot of those old practices." Mrs. X smiled. "I went ahead and put everything we'll need down in the basement—"

"A-ha!" cried Finn.

All the women in the kitchen stared at his outburst.

"It's just…" What was the least embarrassing way out of this? "I assumed this house would have a basement. And it does. So…a-ha."

Kai and her mother simply walked out of the kitchen. Maya hopped off her barstool and patted Finn on the back. "It does my heart good to know that as pretty as you are, you're still a dork."

"Thanks," said Finn.

"Anytime, hot stuff."

The basement was about as dark and dank as a day at the beach. Mrs. X had Kai pull the drapes in front of all the picture windows while she and Maya cleared a coffee table covered in magazines and what looked like small chunks of the Parthenon. Then Mrs. X instructed Finn to move the table so that it sat right in front of a storage closet…a closet whose sliding door was a full-length mirror that reflected the whole room.

"That's a handy thing," Maya said of the doors

as she began to light the white candles and sprinkle her herbs.

"Isn't it?" Mrs. X said proudly. "The mirror not only brightens up the room, it also makes it look twice as big. And it's so feng shui."

Finn glanced at Kai. There would be no hiding in this mirror, for either of them. If things had been different—if he hadn't been the cursed werewolf boy who'd stumbled into her shop and messed up her life—he might have reached out to take her hand or spoken to her telepathically, reassuring her that everything would turn out okay. But things weren't different, so he stayed put, and out of Kai's head.

He couldn't screw up a relationship he never made in the first place, right?

Mrs. X moved Finn and Kai to where she wanted them to stand, and then turned to Maya. "Light it up."

This time, when Maya lit the black candle, the mirror instantly went black. Finn blinked a few times, and when their reflections finally came into focus, he tried not to gasp.

Maya, still crouched beside the coffee table, ready to blow out the black candle at a moment's notice, was now a full-figured woman, with hair that fell over her bronze shoulders all the way to her thighs. It was thick, that hair, and black, waves of black, black as the mirror. Black as her eyes.

Kai's mother had turned into a creature with garnet skin that glowed like an ember and eyes and hair of flames. Kai became an angelic version of her mother and then some: skin made of shadow, golden wolf eyes, writhing snakes for hair, and wings, massive silver-gray wings that seemed to swallow the whole room behind them. Bits of flame winked here and there at the ends of her fingers and the tips of her feathers.

"The Fury." Mrs. X reverently bowed her head to her daughter's image.

Don't look at me, he heard Kai's mind whisper softly. To him? To anyone? It didn't matter.

But you are magnificent, he answered. He might have spotted a tear trying to escape from the corner of her eye, but it evaporated too quickly so close to her mother's flame.

Mrs. X smiled proudly at her Kai before turning to Finn, the half-wolf, with his sick aura. She took in a deep breath and inhaled the curse into her body. Finn watched in the mirror as the sickness disappeared from around his reflection. Suddenly he felt taller. Lighter. Free. The wolf in him wanted to leap for joy and shift and run, but he forced himself to stay.

Now that he had seen the true forms of the powerful women in this room, he planned to do nothing that might anger any of them. The hurt they could put on him would put the entire Kincaid pack to shame.

Kai's mother turned back to the mirror and blew Finn's curse into it, like smoke from a cigar. The mirror turned green, and then black again. All of their images disappeared. One face shimmered up from the depths…a young woman with long, wavy blonde hair, piercing blue eyes, and eyebrows so severely arched that she looked as if she was permanently angry at something. The last time he'd seen her she'd been wearing a black cowboy hat.

"That's her!" said Finn.

"*Heather?*" Kai and Maya said in unison.

"You know her?" Finn asked incredulously.

"Yeah," said Maya. "She goes to our school."

"You've got to be kidding me," breathed Finn.

"Maya," said Mrs. X. "Douse the candle."

Maya did as she was told, quickly extinguishing the flame and the mirror's magical blackness with it. Everyone's reflection returned to their original form...

Except Kai.

As the smoke from the candles lifted, Kai reached down and yanked one of the silver-gray feathers out of her wings.

"For you," she said to Finn.

And then, in human form once again, Kai passed out into his arms.

11

Kai woke up in her bed. Slivers of bright sunlight sliced through the gap in her closed curtains—was she late for school? She shifted slightly and felt a stabbing pain between her shoulder blades.

And then she remembered.

She had turned into the monster. The longer she'd stared at her terrifying image in the spelled mirror, the more she had learned about her true self. She had called on the ancient power in her blood and summoned the Fury into her body almost on instinct. She had communicated with the snakes in her hair, saw history through their eyes and absorbed their teachings. She'd felt passion and pain and the fire in her veins. She knew what vengeance tasted like. She could smell Finn next to her, his fear, for himself and the ones he loved. For his family. For her. And, just like that, she knew how to solve Finn's problem once and for all.

One of her feathers was enough for Finn to exact all the revenge he could ever want. It might have hurt less if she'd asked him to pluck it himself—not that he would have dared. Regardless, a gift was always more powerful for the giving. How he used it…that was all up to him, now. She hoped to god that he chose wisely.

God. *Gods*. Monsters. Whatever.

Kai turned her aching head into the pillow. She now had a different definition for the word Fury. She would learn to handle the powers, but she hoped she never saw the Fury—or turned into her—again.

"He carried you."

The voice was close and slightly muffled, but she'd made out every word.

"Owen?" It took Kai a moment to realize that all of the warmth in the pit of her belly was not entirely of her own making. Owen, in cat form, was curled up against her inside the mess of blankets. Why was he in her room again? How had he gotten in the house at all? If her parents found out she was harboring a pet, they'd kill her.

Worse, when they found out that Owen was more than just a cat, they'd grind her up and brew her for coffee at the diner.

Cat-Owen peeked his cat-head out from the bundle and those golden-green eyes met hers. "The wolf. Finn. He carried you up here and laid you down as if you were the most precious, breakable thing he had ever handled. I had taken up a post in the closet, waiting for you to come back. He knew I was here, but all he said before he left was, 'Take care of her.' Silly mutt. As if I didn't plan on doing that anyway."

Kai almost laughed. It was so like Owen, using his bravado to punctuate an otherwise touchingly chivalrous moment. She absentmindedly scratched the back of his neck and between his ears, just like she used to, until she remembered what he was. She sat up, using the motion to hide how quickly she snatched her hand away.

Just as quickly, Owen shifted into human form. The bed shifted slightly under the new weight of him. "I suppose petting me is strange to you now."

"Pretty much."

"Pity." He stretched out lazily beside her. "I always did enjoy it so."

Kai threw a pillow at his annoyingly beautiful self. "Perv."

Owen caught the pillow and tucked it under his head. "So. What happened with the spell? It was obviously a doozy if it took that much out of you. Tell me every last sordid detail."

Kai shrugged and then winced slightly because she'd forgotten the ache in her back again. She'd yanked out only one feather. If her wings sustained more damage in the future, the pain would be unbearable. "Mom got rid of Finn's curse, as promised. Sucked it up and breathed it out just like a dragon. I've never seen her—or anyone!—do anything like that. It was amazing. She and

Maya used the mirrored closet doors in the basement to scry for the witch who cast Finn's curse. A cool idea, actually."

"And?" he asked eagerly.

"You're never going to believe this. I'm still not sure I do. Turns out it was none other than Horrible Heather."

"Wait...*the* Heather? Our Heather? The Godawful Gothwitch of Harmswood?"

Kai had told Owen more than a few stories about Heather Hayden, head of the mean-girl witch trio at Harmswood. Heather and her two cronettes were all boarding students, richest of the rich and elitist of the elite. Whatever they wanted, they got. Anyone that got in the way, they demolished. Finn hadn't been the first of their casualties, and he surely wouldn't be the last.

"Yup. The one and only Heather." Kai shook her head. "I almost feel like I should have guessed, you know? That witch is a plague to all who know her."

"Ours is a small world."

"You can say that again." Kai leaned back. "You know, I have a vague memory of one of the Gothwitches bragging about going to Nashville for Fall Break, but I never would have put two and two together if it hadn't been for Mom and Maya's mirror."

"I bet that was quite the shock. So, with a mirror that large and powerful on hand...did you happen to see the ara in her true form?"

"I did. She was impressive. And scary. Like Mom in real life, only times a million." Kai remembered the reflection of her mother steeped in power, like an elemental spirit of fire birthed from a volcano. "Have you ever seen a true ara?"

"Once, ages ago. I was very far away. That's about as close as I ever want to be."

"Have you ever seen a Fury?" she asked tentatively. As old as Owen was, and considering that Egypt was also part of Asia Minor, if he'd laid eyes on a Fury back then, there was a good chance it might have been her great-great grandmother.

"Did your parents confirm that's what your

powers are?" he asked.

Kai remembered her mother's awestruck reaction to the snake-haired, winged monster inside her soul. "Pretty much. Now answer my question."

"The answer is no," Owen said casually. "I've only heard stories, and storytelling is a particular talent in that area of the world. But I have been looking for one for a very long time. I've been looking for *you* for a very long time." He sat up slowly. "I wish I could have seen you in that mirror."

"No, you don't." Kai still had difficulty looking at human-Owen and knowing that this was the cat she had poured out her heart to for the last few years. She still felt an odd compulsion to let him curl up in her lap and stroke his hair when she talked to him. She suspected human-Owen would have no problem with that, which is exactly why she didn't make the suggestion. It would only complicate…everything.

She clasped her hands together instead. "I think now would be a good time to tell me why you're here."

"I told you. I was waiting to find out what happened with your cursed boy."

"Not why you're here in my bedroom, Owen. Why you're here *in my life*." All things considered, at some point she did need to come clean with Mom about secretly having a boy in her room…if anyone over a hundred years old could be called a "boy."

"Ah," said Owen. But he didn't seem inclined to say anything more.

Cats.

She wasn't sure if Owen had adopted the mannerisms after he'd become a cat, or if he'd just been that irritating as a human, but now that Kai knew some fraction of her paranormal being was wolven, it made sense why—as much as she loved him—Owen constantly got on her nerves.

"Start with the woman," Kai prompted.

"Who?" Owen asked innocently.

"The incredible, breathtakingly beautiful woman. Start there. Preferably before I lose my patience and sic my furious hair snakes on you."

Owen quickly resumed a sitting position.

"What a horrifying thought."

"Then stop being a pain in the neck and talk already."

"As you wish. Though if you truly suffer from neck pain, I'd suggest hair snakes as a culprit long before me."

"Owen. Enough."

"Fine." He fluffed three pillows and placed them between his back and the headboard. Then he removed one. Then he wriggled his butt a few times and put the pillow back behind his head. When Kai was well and truly exasperated, Owen folded his arms across his chest and began.

"I was orphaned young, and my only distant relation was an eccentric baron with a penchant for archaeology. It was the turn of the century, the age of Carnarvon and Carter, the height of popularity for Egyptian antiquities. The apex of aristocratic luxury was literally digging for treasure in a sandbox."

"So he took you in? The baron?"

"He did. For all his harebrained schemes, the

baron was a kind man. But as a poor relation, I was little more than a servant. I did far more fetching and carrying than I did scraping and brushing, but no nannies or governesses or headmasters were bothered on my account."

"Did the baron discover anything on his digs?" asked Kai.

"Nothing of particular historical import," said Owen. "Probably for the best, judging by the fate of Carter and his crew after disturbing Tutankhamen's eternal rest."

The Curse of the Pharaohs was still heavily debated in the human world after all these years. "Mom always says curses are not to be taken lightly," said Kai. "But the ancient ones do seem worse than any that have been cast since."

"You're telling me," said the boy who'd been transformed by a Sphinx.

"Right," Kai said sheepishly. "Sorry."

Owen continued his story. "While the baron's discoveries never amounted to anything that would alarm the Antiquities Commission, something else did catch his eye. Or, rather, someone else."

"The beautiful woman!" guessed Kai. "Finally. What sort of supernatural was she? Because I'm guessing she had powers if she factors into this."

"You guessed right. She was an arachne."

Kai didn't remember all the myths they'd covered in the fourth grade at Harmswood, but Arachne was one of the more famous. "The woman who was cursed into a spider by Athena because she wove so well?"

"That's the one. Apparently, Arachne's descendants not only inherited her deadly good looks, they also got her bitterness and desire for revenge."

Kai smirked. "With good reason." In the myth, Arachne was an expert weaver who'd boasted about her talents to the world by challenging Athena to a weave-off...which Arachne promptly won. Instead of conceding gracefully, Athena turned Arachne into a spider so that she could go on weaving forever, to punish her for her hubris. "I always liked Athena, but

I'll be the first to admit that what she did to Arachne was not her finest hour." Arachne's story was a warning to the god-fearing world at the time: if you happened to have an awesome talent, it was best to keep your mouth shut about it.

Needless to say, Bellamy and Athena would probably not have been friends.

"This arachne essentially offered me the world if I retrieved the feather of a Fury for her. A tempting reward for a young man with so few prospects. Rumors of a Fury had risen from the north, tales of one forced out of hiding by the atrocities happening in the Ottoman Empire. By the time I tracked her down, what was left of her family had either been killed or exiled. At which point the arachne tricked me into staring at the Sphinx so that I could walk the world as a cat, ageless, tracking the Fury and her descendants until I finally found one and killed her."

"What?" Kai was sure she must have heard that part wrong. "*Killed* her?"

Owen shrugged. "Furies don't exactly have a reputation for being generous. I was told it was the only way to get my hands on a feather."

Kai froze for a moment, stunned. Owen had been sent *to kill her*. He hadn't yet, which was certainly a good sign. Moreover, the tale about killing a Fury to retrieve a feather was completely false—Kai had proven that last night. Of course, Kai could easily imagine a fight to the death if a Fury decided she wasn't ready to part with a feather quite so willingly. "Have you ever killed anyone before?"

"No." Owen yawned. "Figured I would cross that bridge when I came to it."

How could he be so casual about this? That was just so…Owen. Kai looked at him sternly. "And now that you've come to it?"

Owen met her eyes with no fear. "Truth be told, I didn't count on falling in love with the Fury and making her my best friend. There's no way I'm killing her now."

Leave it to Owen to be the laziest assassin in a hundred years. But lucky for her! Kai relaxed in relief. "So what happens when the arachne finds out?"

"You mean, *if* she finds out? If, after all this time, she or her descendants are even still around to care?" Owen grinned wryly. "I'll cross that bridge when I come to it."

Once again, the answer was such an Owen-type answer, she almost groaned. "You know," she said, "you shouldn't stare into my eyes for too long. I could turn you to stone. I do have snakes for hair. And a lot of other crazy latent powers, I'm sure."

Owen's grin spread across his face. "Don't flatter yourself, love. You're no Sphinx." Instead of looking away, he only came closer. "But *you* might worry. I've heard that if you stare into the eyes of a cat-shifter long enough, you can see into fairyland."

"Really?" Kai concentrated on Owen's green eyes, and the explosion of gold inside them.

Only the very brave are willing to take the risk, Owen teased inside her head.

Too bad I'm a such a scaredy cat, Kai joked in return.

And then Owen kissed her.

His lips were soft and sweet, gentle and comfortable. It was quick. It was nice.

But it wasn't Finn.

Owen reached up and smoothed the furrow in her brow. "That bad, huh?"

Kai tried to smile and failed miserably. "It should be you," she said. "We've known each other for years. We're best friends, despite the fact that you were essentially sent here to kill me."

"Technically, we're friends *because* I was sent here."

"Semantics!" This time, Kai did groan. "See what I mean? We constantly drive each other up the wall, but only because we love each other. But you and me...romantically? It just doesn't feel right."

"I respect your wishes, so I'll save you the breath of arguing about this one. But I had to try." Owen pulled her close, patting her hair in much the same way she pet him as a cat. "Do you think if I had appeared to you in human form, before you met the wolf, that it might have worked out between us?"

"Maybe," she said into his chest. "I don't know."

But she did know. If Owen had appeared to her years, months, even weeks ago in that beautiful bedraggled human form of his, she would have fallen in love with him at first sight. And then Finn would have come along anyway and blown it all apart, ruining everything between them. This was better. This way, Kai and Owen could stay friends forever. And Finn would just have to deal with it.

Kai kissed Owen on the cheek as she pulled away. "I just don't understand. Why am I so attracted to Finn when I already love you?"

Oddly enough, Owen had an answer to the question that had been bothering her for days. "Because he makes your blood boil. He makes your heart sing. Your mutual canine aspects howl for each other. You know, deep down in your true self, that the two of you could be something, something big, and you desperately want to find out. I haven't met anyone in the last hundred years who wouldn't be tempted by that."

"Point for the cat," she said.

"On top of which, you're a Fury. Furies may enjoy normal human comforts from time to time...even need them...but they do not crave them. They crave fire. And, as much as it breaks my heart to say it, that wolf definitely sets you on fire. I suspect he might very well be your soulmate."

"Oh, please," said Kai. Bellamy believed in soulmates. Read every book and watched every cheesy movie in existence. Kai indulged her, but she'd always thought the notion incredibly narrow-minded. "Even if romantic soulmates existed, nobody finds theirs in high school, before they've even had a chance to live their life yet."

Owen shrugged. "Someone with a curse might."

Another point for Owen. Kai closed her eyes and shook her head. "I am going to kill Heather."

"Love, you're a Fury. You want vengeance?" Owen snapped. "You got it." He stared at his fingers. "Weird. Been a long time since I've done that. Aren't opposable thumbs grand?"

But Kai wasn't listening. She thought back to the feather. "Vengeance. Oh, Owen...I...may have already taken it."

Finn could use that feather to force Heather to take back her spell. He could turn it on its head and give the curse straight back to her. Kai had given him the power to exact justice—and his revenge—in whatever way he saw fit. Ways possibly even more horrible than she could imagine.

"What do you mean?" asked Owen.

"Maya reminded me that the Furies had the potential to be benevolent instead of terrible, so I decided that was what I wanted to be. A good person with benevolent powers. Vengeance keeps evil out in the universe, perpetuating chaos by following one horrible act with another, and then another. We've learned enough in history to know that revenge is never the answer. But justice...justice isn't so bad. Right?"

"Kai," said Owen. "What did you do?"

"I gave Finn one of my feathers," she said.

Owen froze.

"I wasn't thinking. I mean, I thought it would make it possible for him to set things right between them, but I didn't really have time to process it much beyond that because I passed out from the pain."

"Oh wow." Owen let himself fall back onto the bed.

"I trust Finn to do the right thing," she said. "He wouldn't turn the curse back on Heather, would he? He's not that kind of person. The universe wouldn't make a horrible person my soulmate, would it?"

"Kai, it's more than just the curse. That feather is essentially an eye-for-an-eye. Heather's curse *killed* his pack-brother. Finn could use that feather to kill her right back. He could use it to kill anyone." He turned to Kai. "You handed your lust-buddy a free pass for justifiable homicide."

Kai started to shiver and wrapped her arms around herself. "This is exactly what I didn't want to be."

"Okay, let's try thinking about this from a

different angle," said Owen. "Right now, you haven't done anything but put the potential out into the world."

So far, this new angle wasn't helping. "That's like saying 'You only made the bomb; you didn't set it.'"

"True. But even if you made the bomb and set the bomb and put the bomb on a train and sent it to Washington, it hasn't exploded yet."

"Unless you're about to tell me that you have the Avengers or the Justice League on speed dial, I don't see how this is helpful."

Owen tapped his forehead. "Reach out to him. From in here. Tell him to...I don't know...wait to confront Heather until you talk to him. Tell him whatever you want, just as long as he stops what he's doing before he knows what he's getting into."

"I don't know," said Kai. "I've never tried telepathy across long distances before. It might not work."

Owen took her hand. "Kai, if that wolf is your soulmate, I'd be pretty surprised if it didn't."

Still dubious, Kai closed her eyes and took a deep

break. She tried to quiet her mind, concentrating on Finn. He suddenly appeared in her mind, at her window, and once again he grabbed her and kissed her. Kai's cheeks instantly flushed.

"Whoa." Owen must have felt the rising heat of her through their joined hands.

FINN, she called out in her mind. *FINN? ARE YOU THERE?*

She didn't hear him answer her, but she felt his presence. He could hear her. He was listening.

FINN, WAIT FOR ME. PLEASE.

"Kai, honey?" Mom's call from downstairs broke Kai's concentration and her eyes snapped open. "Are you awake yet? We need to talk."

Kai hopped off the bed and opened the door a crack. "Coming, Mom."

"Did it work?" asked Owen.

Kai nodded. Her head throbbed faintly between her eyebrows. "I think so."

"So are you going over there?"

"In a little bit," said Kai. "First, I'm going to introduce you to my family."

12

Finn sat in the woods just beyond Hank and Ivy's backyard and stared at the feather.

Even with his curse removed, however temporarily, he didn't feel entirely comfortable inside the house. Hank and Ivy and Charlie were his blood, but Finn still felt like he hadn't earned a place in their pack. Charlie's room was little more than a borrowed bed to him. Here on the rocks and the moss by the babbling brook, hidden by the thicket of trees: this was his place. He had a stash of food and books, dense brush to hide his shifted form, and a soft place to lay his head, be he human or wolf. Barring a few more personal items, this new place was a lot like his spot back in Tennessee.

The forest was where the wild, outcast things belonged.

The silver-gray feather in his hand was like liquid mercury frozen into a thing of power. Amazing how something so light could be so...heavy. He could almost smell the forceful magic it possessed. He never would have imagined that one small town girl's nature might contain such secrets.

Had fate really forced them to cross paths? After Tor's death, the machines of the universe knew how rightfully Finn deserved vengeance. But what had Kai deserved? Certainly not him. What did he know besides a bunch of pretty words from a handful of books? What skills did he have? He couldn't even change the oil on Bellamy's pumpkinmobile. What was he good for?

No soul as kind and generous as Kai deserved someone as worthless as Finn.

He spun the quill between his fingers, watched the down on it flutter in the breeze. Kai had given the feather to him so that he could force the witch to remove her curse, once and for all. Even if it happened that easily…then what? Would Hank and Ivy invite him to stay? Would they find a place for him here? And moreover: did he want to remain here in this strange, small town? Did he want to spend the rest of his life trying to maintain his distance from the girl he wanted more than anything on this earth?

Could he imagine the rest of his life without her?

As much as he didn't want to admit it to himself, he knew the answer to that last question. He wanted to be in Kai's life. Needed to. Maybe when all this curse business was said and done she might be willing to give him a second chance. Maybe they could start over. He could re-introduce himself and they could go on a date and make awkward conversation and hold hands and all that other crap that normal teenagers did.

Like he'd told Maya: maybe, in this crazy little town, horses really could fly.

But first he had to deal with the witch.

Maya had told him that Heather was a boarding

student at Harmswood, so she'd be easy enough to find. What he wasn't so sure about was how to get there. His days of shifting into a wolf and scampering about the countryside whenever he wanted were over. Nor did he want to bother Ivy about giving him a ride. He could really use one of those imaginary flying horses right about now. Or a bike.

He bet Charlie had a bike he could borrow.

Inspired, Finn hopped off the rock on all fours and began his run back to the house.

Finn?

Finn shifted without warning, face planting into a pile of dried leaves. He rolled over, spat the dirt and detritus out of his mouth, and rubbed his raw palms on his jeans. Kai's voice in his head had caught him off guard, so much so that he'd become human.

That was new.

She said something else, but he couldn't make it out. How far away was she? Two miles? More? And how in the moon was it possible for him to hear her over such a distance? He closed his eyes, turned his head into the cool breeze, tried to still his breath and the pounding of his heart so that he might hear her better.

Finn, wait for me. Please.

He would have done anything for her…but the "please" broke his heart. Their mind-to-mind contact now seemed far less intimate once such formality was imposed.

I will, he answered, though he wasn't sure she'd heard him.

He would wait for her forever.

Finn walked to the front of the house and sat by the mailbox until he saw her turn down the street. "Thank you for waiting," she said as she hopped off her bike.

"No problem." Finn looked up at the house and decided that he didn't want to have their conversation right there in the driveway. "Come on back. I want to show you something."

"Okay."

He almost held his hand out to her, then

remembered his promise to stay away and shoved his fists in the pockets of his jacket instead. He led her around the side of the house, into the woods, and down to the stream. She followed dutifully and without complaint. When he pulled the hedge aside to allow entrance into his spot she raised an eyebrow at him, but said nothing as she ducked inside.

"Oh, Finn," she gasped. "This is beautiful."

Finn tried to see his spot through someone else's eyes. "It's nothing compared to the space I had in Tennessee, but it's nice enough."

Kai immediately plopped down on the moss and soft brush he'd collected and leaned back against one of the stones. "I see why you like being out here. It's so comfortable. And peaceful."

Finn wasn't sure what reaction he'd expected from Kai, but this wasn't it. "I'm surprised to hear you say that."

"Why? Because I'm a teenager in the internet generation? Give me some credit. Besides," she nodded to the small cache of items nestled in the rocks, "I'm surprised you like Hank the Cowdog and the Wimpy Kid."

Finn laughed a little and sat beside her on the bank. "Purloined from the library of one Charlie Merrow. They're actually rather fun. It's been a while since…"

Finn didn't know how to finish the sentence. On the one hand, Kai was incredibly easy to talk to. On the other hand, there were certain events in his past—and the feelings that came with them—that he wanted to communicate to her, but he still wasn't sure how to put them into words. If only he were Shakespeare.

Heck, even Wimpy Kid was more eloquent than he'd been lately.

Kai filled in the silence for him. "You've got a sitting area, a water feature, a fire pit, and decent cover from the sky. This is so great. It's like a blanket fort without blankets. Like a treehouse beneath the trees."

"You sound like a real estate agent."

"Please. I would never sell this place. I love it."

"So what was it you wanted to talk to me about?

I assume that's why you asked me to wait for you."

"I'm still amazed that you heard me," said Kai. "These powers are going to take some getting used to. They're so…overwhelming. And dangerous. Like that feather."

Finn pulled the feather from his jacket and set it on the ground between them. "I get the sense that this object is a lot more than I bargained for," he said. "Much like its owner."

"Point for the wolf," she said softly, almost to herself. "Okay, yes, I'm here to discuss the feather, but first I want to say something else."

"Go on."

"It's about Owen."

Finn clenched his teeth. "I take it that this is the rest of the story you didn't tell your friends in the greenhouse."

"Sort of," said Kai. "It's complicated. And there are a lot of details Owen hasn't shared yet."

Finn snorted. "Why am I not surprised?"

"I said yet," emphasized Kai. "I'm giving him a chance to fill in the blanks on his own time, when he's comfortable enough to tell me. He was trapped in the body of a cat a century ago by a horrible person…and I am not a horrible person, so I'm not going to pressure him. He's essentially been waiting all these years to find me."

"You mean, find someone with your unique powers." Finn almost spat the words.

"Yes," said Kai. "But that is why we met several years ago, and since then we've become friends. Good friends. He promised to hide the knowledge of my existence from the people who captured him, and I trust him. Because I love him."

Finn knew there was more she wasn't telling him, on top of what the cat hadn't told her, but it all fell away when she'd made her declaration of love. Love. She threw the word around so casually. Finn had not been raised to be so generous with his affection.

Finn had made it clear that he would not pursue Kai, but it felt like he'd just lost her all the same. "I hope you're very happy together," he said stoically.

Kai sighed with her whole body, and then an avalanche of words fell from her mouth. "Look. I do love Owen. I will probably always love Owen. He's one of my very best friends. But I happen to be *in love* with you. You are aware that there's a difference, right? If you and I are going to try and make this work, you're going to have to be okay with the fact that Owen is in my life. I'm serious. That's a deal breaker. Okay?"

Once again, Finn was stunned into silence. Love. In love. Of course there was a difference, not that he'd ever had a reason to differentiate between the two. He still wasn't sure about love like authors described in books: deep and abiding, born out of trust and respect. He suspected that he would love Kai at some point…probably soon, and probably forever. But *in love*?

Oh, yes. He was absolutely in love with her.

Finn couldn't think of a response that would convey his feelings better than a kiss, but Kai held up her hand as he leaned toward her.

"It's not that I don't want to," she said at his

tortured expression. "It's just…I think we should keep our distance until this whole curse thing is done for good. This is the third necklace my mother's given me, and I'd like for it to stay in one piece."

Finn saw it now, the bright blue evil eye charm at her throat. As she moved, he could have sworn it winked at him.

Finn smiled devilishly. "As you wish."

"Now, about the feather…"

"Exactly how much of the world can I blow up with it?" he asked plainly.

"How big a sociopath are you?" she asked in return.

"None at all," he answered. He'd grown up beside enough sociopaths, ones that would have taken this feather and reached maximum havoc, just because they could. Ones that had beaten him and left him for dead rather than wait to hear his side of the story.

"Good news for the world, then," she said. "It appears my powers are…incredibly potent. Turns out I'm a Fury. Ancient Greek Angel of Vengeance, essentially. Runs in the family."

"And those powers are…?"

Kai counted them off on her fingers. "So far: making things hot; telepathic communication, which is easier with shifters, apparently; and shedding apocalyptic feathers. Oh"—she snapped—"and never wanting to look in a magic mirror."

Finn remembered the magnificent figure of her in that magic mirror and his whole body ached to worship her. "I can tell you how beautiful you are, if you like."

She blushed, an act that now would always remind him of the magical fire banked inside her. "I'll take a raincheck," she said. "Finn, I don't know why I gave you that feather. I mean, I do—you obviously deserved it—but the act was more instinctual than anything. I had no idea of the scope of what I was handing over, which my mother helped make clear to me once I regained consciousness. She wants to call Harmswood and set up a meeting with Heather at the house, so you can confront her in a safe, controlled environment. And then we will all deal with the feather, together."

Everything she was telling him made sense. It was the logical, intelligent thing to do. Which made his desire to do no such thing borderline insane.

"No," he said.

"No?"

"That reckless witch doesn't deserve a safe, controlled environment. She doesn't deserve a heads up, or a wise council. She deserves this"—he snatched the feather up and shoved it back in his jacket pocket—"and I'm going to give it to her. Right now."

Kai stood with him, and Finn braced himself. She would yell at him now, call him names, beg him to reconsider. She would reason with him and convince him to be sensible. But she did none of those things.

"Fine," she said. "I'm coming with you."

If it wasn't for her recent rule of distance, Finn would have caught her up in his arms, spun her around, and kissed her again. That one gesture summed up all the faith she had in him to not screw this up. Kai Xanthopoulos really was one remarkable girl, which made him one very lucky wolf. "This being in love thing isn't half bad, is it?"

Kai shrugged nonchalantly, but smiled at him all the same. "I'll let you know when I get back from following a boy to the end of the world."

Finn held his hand out before her. "Lead the way."

He grabbed Charlie's bike out of the garage—it was a bit small, but it had a solid frame and sturdy tires. Together they biked down one street after another, wind in their faces, no sound but the crunch of dried leaves beneath their wheels. The air became chillier as the sun began to set. Finn worried about Kai in her thin jacket for the briefest of moments before remembering that the ability to kindle fire was literally at her fingertips. What fun it would be to run with her across snow-swept hills.

If he stayed in the Falls after all this was done.

They took a winding road up a wooded hill that the trees had called home for centuries. In the spring and summer, Finn guessed that the leaves and underbrush were so impressive that even cars might find the road impassible in spots. Now, with autumn giving way to winter, the bare limbs afforded glimpses of wildlife, more trees, and more hills beyond.

Eventually, they came to a massive gate that loomed above them with ominous wrought-iron majesty, but Finn could tell it was just for show. There was no connected fence around the perimeter, for there was no need.

"Woe to all who dare trespass here," he said.

"Exactly." Kai took her bike off-road and led him around the side of the gate.

The school itself was almost as massive as the forest that surrounded it. Finn might have called it a castle—and parts of it were—but it looked more like a collage amalgam of maybe a dozen different architectural styles all mashed together and piled on top of one another, from columned ancient ruins to stiff-peaked Victorian mansions. The grounds beyond the main school building were filled with gardens and playing fields and outbuildings and no doubt even more beyond that.

"Have I seen a structure like this before?" he asked as he took it all in.

"There's a place on the west coast called the Winchester Mystery House. Sort of like Harmswood's lesser non-magical cousin." Kai did not enter through the front door, but walked her bike around until they reached a stone patio. Despite the season, the urns that lined the patio overflowed with blooming flowers of every sort. At the door, Kai pulled a small, laminated card from her pocket and inserted it in the reader beside the handle. Her school ID.

Finn never would have gotten into this fortress without her help. He opened his mouth to thank her for it, but she put her finger over her lips.

"This is the girls' wing," she whispered. "Boys aren't supposed to be here. So keep your voice down."

I keep forgetting that you and I don't need voices, he projected to her.

She smiled at him. *So do I.*

Finn could happily bask in the sight of that smile for the rest of his days. *Let's do this.*

The stairs are this way, she said. Heart racing, Finn followed her around the corner...

...and almost ran straight into the teacher that was waiting for them.

The woman folded her arms over her ample bosom and clucked at both of them. "Oh no, no," she said. "I'm afraid this will never do."

13

They followed Professor Blake up a different flight of grand, hand-carved stairs and down several more corridors until they reached the door of her office: a massive oaken thing with leaves framing it in detailed relief. That door was a masterpiece of craftsmanship...and one that Kai could never look at without feeling as though she were in trouble.

Like now.

She didn't have to be telepathic to know that Finn was fuming as he was marched to the office, or that—once Professor Blake opened the door and they saw Heather sitting there—he was ready to turn full wolf and rip the Gothwitch's head off with his bare teeth.

Heather, as usual, looked like she'd stepped straight out of a comic book. She was dressed all in black from head to toe: black top, short black skirt, black kid boots, black choker, even a black headband in her straight blond hair. It occurred to Kai that Finn's clothes were all black too, but the shade looked natural on him. Not quite so...pretentious.

"That's funny," Heather said with great condescension as they entered the office, "I don't remember ordering delivery, but now I'm suddenly craving pizza. Is Mummy's Diner reading minds now?"

"As a matter of fact, I have a knuckle sandwich here with your name on it," said Kai.

That's my girl, she heard Finn say.

"Now, children," said Professor Blake, "and yes, I will call you children, for that is what you're acting like. Please, have a seat."

Finn growled through bared teeth. "I'll stand, if it's all the same."

"It is not," said Professor Blake, and with the slightest flick of her finger, Finn plopped down into the nearest chair like a tossed rag doll.

Sorry, Kai sent to him. She wasn't sure if she was apologizing for them getting caught, or for not being able to warn him about Professor Blake's power, or for the load of trouble they were about to be in, but she guessed he'd figure that out.

The only indication the professor gave that she knew words were being exchanged between Kai and Finn was a slight raise of her eyebrows. She settled into the oversized leather chair behind her desk. The desk was covered in clutter: stacks of papers, pens, quills, a stuffed raven, a bleached human skull. "Young man, I am Theodosia Persimmon Blake, Head Witch of Harmswood this school year."

Now back in control of his faculties, Finn scooted his chair closer to Kai. "Finn Kincaid, ma'am. I'd say I'm pleased to meet you, but under the circumstances—"

Professor Blake slid her glasses down her nose and peered at Finn over them. "And what circumstances are those, exactly?"

"About a month ago, my brother Tor and I ran into this witch"—he pointed at Heather—"at a club in Nashville, and she cursed him. Cursed both of us."

Heather waved a hand dismissively. "Big deal. I curse a lot of people."

Professor Blake scowled at Heather. "Young lady, cursing is a matter that we take very seriously here at Harmswood, as you well know."

Heather immediately tried to backpedal under Professor Blake's scrutiny. "If I recall, he deserved it for trying to force himself on me."

Kai suspected that if Finn had the ability to breathe fire, he would have. "Tor hit on a pretty girl in a crowded bar," she said. "He did not deserve to die for that."

"What?" Heather's fingers flew to her lips and all the blood drained from her face.

So she hadn't known about Tor's death, or her role in it. Until that moment, Kai hadn't been sure. Heather often took it upon herself to be malicious, but Kai was pretty sure Heather wouldn't have killed someone on purpose.

Pretty sure.

"Since you cursed me as well with your terrible words, I'm here so that you can remove that curse." Slowly, Finn pulled Kai's feather from his jacket pocket. "And I've brought this to make sure it happens."

"A feather?" Heather scoffed. "You must be joking."

Professor Blake's already solemn face became grim at the presentation of the feather—she obviously knew what it was, and what it meant. She glanced at Kai, but addressed Finn. "Young man, what are your intentions with that?"

"Honestly?" Finn shook his head. "I don't know."

"Would you allow me to present you with a few options?"

At that moment, Kai wanted to hug the woman. In the absence of her mother, Professor Blake was one of the people most likely to know about ancient powers and their consequences. Kai nodded to Finn.

"Please," he said.

"The feather of a Fury has the power to dole out ultimate justice," the Head Witch said in her most professor-like tone. "You would be well within your rights to demand a life for a life."

"What?" screeched Heather. "He can't——"

Professor Blake pointed at Heather and her lips clamped shut. Kai did not deny herself the small amount of glee that swelled inside her.

"By taking the life of that witch, the curse would automatically be broken. You would walk away from here, free and clear."

A solitary tear escaped down one of Heather's cheeks. Kai was mildly surprised that the witch even could cry.

"And if I don't want to become a murderer?" he asked.

"You could ask the witch to remove your curse and simply destroy the feather." The professor clasped her hands together authoritatively. "Her fate rests in your hands. Quite literally."

What should I do? he asked Kai through their mental bond.

Kai did not envy Finn's position, but she was determined to remain beside him. There were so many things she wanted to say to him, so much advice she wanted to give…but ultimately, the decision was his to make.

You should finish up here so you can ask me out on a date, she answered.

As she'd hoped, Finn's ears perked up at her glib reply. "I would like the witch to remove my curse please," he said to the professor.

The Head Witch pointed again to Heather whose now-open lips burst out with, "But I don't know how!"

"I will teach you," said Professor Blake. "After all, that's why I'm here, isn't it? To remove this young man's curse, you must apologize."

Heather looked overjoyed.

"*Sincerely* apologize," the professor added.

Heather reined in the excitement over her good fortune. "Finn Kincaid, I sincerely apologize for cursing you and your brother. What I did was out of spite, but I had no idea—" Heather's sudden modesty surprised Kai. The more she spoke, the more…human she seemed. "I truly meant no real harm. I am so, so sorry for your loss."

Professor Blake nodded. "And thusly, your curse is broken."

Finn could hardly believe it. "Forever?"

"Forever," said the professor. "Now, the standard punishment for a witch in a case like this is to be stripped of her powers for five years. What do you say to that?"

This time, Heather wisely kept her mouth shut of her own accord.

"If she has no powers, can she learn how to avoid such a mistake in the future?"

"No she cannot," said the professor. "On top of which, at her age, there would be no graduation from this school, and no possibility of subsequent collegiate study."

And there it was. As badly as Heather deserved vengeance, Kai did not believe that Finn could end her life, or ruin it. Perhaps if Kai hadn't been there, he might have acted differently…an outcome Kai was happy that she would never know.

"Then I will leave her magical education in your very capable hands," said Finn. "As for her fate…I will leave that in hers." Finn took Heather's hand, opened it up, and placed the feather inside it. "Destroying this would be too easy. Instead, I want you to have to take care of this as if your life depends on it. Because it does."

Leaving the feather intact meant that Finn could still return and exact his vengeance at any time. Plus, Finn knew that if Heather used the feather for harm in any way, the coven would strip her powers in the blink of an eye.

"An interesting choice, young man." said Professor Blake. "And with that, justice has been served."

Heather stared at the feather in her hand as if it were a scorpion. "But…aren't you going to make him destroy it? He has to, right? He can't leave me with this!"

"My dear," said Professor Blake. "He already did. It was not the path I wish he had taken, of course, but the decision was not mine to make." She rose from her chair, stepped around her desk, and plucked the feather from Heather's hand. "Now, if you don't mind, I'll be locking this up in the Harmswood vault on your behalf. It would never do to have such an object of power freely mucking about this place." She pointed the feather at Heather. "But do not mistake me, young lady, this does not free you from responsibility."

"Yes, professor," Heather muttered. Her cold blue eyes shot daggers at Kai over the feather.

"And now I will bid you good night, Miss Hayden," said the professor.

"Just me? What about them?" she asked of Finn and Kai.

"We still have matters to discuss. Matters beyond the one that pertained to you."

Heather rose slowly, as if she meant to, rather than being summarily dismissed. It was a move that Kai had seen Owen make a thousand times— Heather's effort paled in comparison to the cat-shifter.

Heather, who no doubt noticed Kai's slight grin, leaned over her chair as she made her way to the door. "You'll pay for this, Kalliope," she hissed under her breath, but not quietly enough.

"I wouldn't make that one angry if I were you, dear." Professor Blake smiled beatifically. "The feather came from her."

Kai beamed as the professor all but slammed the door in Heather's face.

"Oh, that felt good," said Professor Blake. "Not that either of you heard me say that."

"Yes, professor," Kai said at the same time Finn replied, "Yes, ma'am."

Horrible Heather had been left contemplating her mistakes, with the knowledge that every witch in the Nocturne Falls coven would be keeping one eye on her. Best of all, Finn was no longer cursed.

Professor Blake moved to return to her chair. In doing so, she jostled a perilous stack of papers. Folders slid in all directions, including one that knocked the skull right off the desk.

"Alas, poor Yorick!" cried the professor.

Finn deftly caught the skull in one hand and returned it to the Professor with a flourish. "I knew him, Horatio."

Hamlet again, thought Kai, as she knelt to collect the scattered papers. When she rose, she saw Finn and the professor exchange a smile.

"I've spoken at length with your cousin," said Professor Blake. "She posed some questions regarding your enrollment here."

"Oh?" asked Finn. He clearly had no idea Ivy had done such a thing.

"I admit to having my misgivings, based on what I learned of your past...and recent mischief." She was referring to Finn's police chase down Black Cat Boulevard, of course. Kai wondered if she knew about the kiss, too.

"However," the professor went on, "in light of your actions here this evening, I am inclined to extend an offer of admission, should you care to accept it." Finn opened his mouth to speak, but the professor held up a hand. "Take some time. Discuss it with your cousin. Should you choose to accept, we will discuss the possibility of financial aid, as well as room and board. But for now, think it over. Harmswood is not just any school, and this is not a decision to be made lightly." She opened an ornate metal box on her desk and dropped the Fury feather inside it. "You've made enough tough decisions for one day."

Finn stood and offered the professor his hand. "Thank you, ma'am."

"Call me Professor Blake," she said as she shook it. "And now I will bid you both good night. I will leave it to Kai to show you out."

"Yes, professor," Kai said dutifully, and they turned to the door.

"And Kai?"

Kai froze. She should have known she wouldn't be able to leave this office without some form of punishment. "Yes, professor?"

"I look forward to your training. It should be very...enlightening. For us both."

Kai wasn't sure if she was on the verge of bursting into tears or laughter. "Yes. Thank you, professor.

Good night."

She took Finn's hand, dragged him out of the professor's office, and raced down the halls. She couldn't get out of Harmswood fast enough. Once out the door they hopped on their bikes, grabbed the nearly frozen handlebars, and sped back down the road through the now-dark woods.

Kai concentrated so hard on keeping her wheels on the winding road that she was halfway down the hill before she realized Finn was no longer behind her. She found him about half a mile back. Charlie's bike had fallen by the wayside, and Finn was doubled over on the road as if he'd been stabbed in the stomach.

Kai leapt off her bike and rushed to his side. "Finn?"

He frantically beat at his chest, gasping for air. He made as if to scream, but there was no sound, as if his body was sobbing with no tears. He tore off his jacket; she helped him when his arms got tangled in the sleeves. He looked at her then, his face wrecked.

Kai had never seen a panic attack in real life before, but she guessed it looked a lot like this.

She pulled him into her arms there on the road, hugged him tightly and gently rubbed his back until he calmed down enough to catch his breath. She used the heat of her Fury magic to keep his body warm in the chill of the night, being careful not to overdo it—the last thing she needed was to set the hill on fire and burn Harmswood to the ground before Finn had a chance to make up his mind about the place.

She wasn't sure what had triggered this sudden emotional overflow, but after what Finn had been through, she suspected it was a long time coming. She managed to coax his large body to the side of the road—not that many folks had business coming and going from Harmswood this late at night, but better safe than sorry. She propped him up on the trunk of a fallen tree, and then went to fetch the bikes. When she returned to him, he was significantly calmer.

"I'm sorry," he said. "I don't know——"

"'Proclaim no shame,'" she quoted to him,

hoping for a smile.

"Can I confess something stupid?" he said quietly.

Kai hopped up onto the tree trunk beside him. "Confess away."

"In a weird way, that stupid curse was my last link to Tor. Now that it's gone…"

"…it feels like he's left you all over again. Oh, Finn. I'm so sorry."

Finn shrugged. "It's not like I was going to ask to keep it. A curse is a pretty crappy memento. I just…never expected I would hurt this badly after it was over."

Kai turned her face up to the star-filled sky. "I'm sure Tor would agree that you made the right choice."

"Yeah."

He hadn't put the jacket back on, so Kai rubbed his back again, making sure to keep him warm. The street lamps along this road were few and far between; the only light that fell upon them in this spot was cast by the moon. Under other circumstances it might have been a spooky setting, but Finn had lived in the woods all his life. Kai could sense that this conversation about Tor was best had here, a place that was both secret and safe.

"I feel obliged to say all the cliche stuff right now," she said.

"Like what?"

"Like, that Tor will always remain in your heart and your memories. That he would encourage you to take the rest of this life you have and live it to the fullest, for his sake."

Finn huffed. "And what sort of life is that? Surviving, getting revenge, and ridding myself of this curse...all of that has consumed me. Now that I don't have to run anymore, I feel lost in this new place with no idea what to do."

"Have you considered piracy?" she joked.

Finn looked her curiously. "What?"

Kai realized her mistake. "Sorry, it's a reference to the end of *The Princess Bride*. One of my favorite movies...but one I'm guessing you probably haven't seen."

"No," said Finn. "It's funny; I was thinking about that book earlier. But I don't remember that line being anywhere at the end."

"That's right, I forgot it was a book," said Kai. "How does the book end?"

He smirked. "With a reminder that life isn't fair, it's just fairer than death."

Kai wrinkled her nose. "Well, that sounds slightly more optimistic than *Hamlet*, at any rate."

Finn slowly reached out for her hand, slid his fingers in between hers. They were cold, so she warmed them. It was a small part of her nature to be sure, but it felt good to finally have a power that was reliably useful.

"Thank you, Kai."

The tone of his voice broke her heart all over again.

"For what?" she asked. "For sneaking you into the girls' wing? For getting you out of trouble with the Head Witch? For unknowingly handing you a free pass to murder someone? Oh! I know…for not pressing charges that day in the police station."

Finn squeezed her hand. "For all of that and more. For being you."

Kai squeezed his hand back and waited, but Finn made no move to be more intimate with her. The curse was gone and they were all alone beneath a gorgeous moon. Her heart began to beat a little faster. He needed comfort right now. Her mind should be on Finn's lost brother, not on his lips, or his breath, or the tight muscles in his back, or the weight of his hand in hers. He'd kissed her before, in far less perfect conditions. Surely the big bad wolf wasn't afraid of her *now*. Was he?

"So, do you think you're going to stay?" she asked him.

"You know, I've never officially been to school," he admitted. "There was an aunt who came around and taught us a few things when I was a cub, but the older boys chased her away."

Kai turned her head to him and her dark hair whipped across her cheek. "Is she the one who taught you to read?"

"Yes, thankfully. After that, I taught myself

whatever I could."

"I like the learning part, too," said Kai. "The society, on the other hand, not so much."

"Is Harmswood really that bad?"

Kai let out a small laugh. "Horrible Heather's just the tip of the iceberg. It's a jungle in there."

"Well," said Finn. "Lucky for me, the jungle is something I know how to deal with."

"And do you still want to try this thing?" she asked innocently. "The me and you thing?"

Finn shook his head but did not release her hand. "I don't deserve you."

"Oh, I'm almost positive you don't."

That remark made him turn to her, and she smiled at him. If only she knew how to make him kiss her! How had she caused it to happen before? Because his tormented wolf self was maybe the most achingly beautiful thing she had ever seen, and she definitely wanted to kiss him *right now*.

Then you should, he said in her head.

Kai grimaced. "I really need to learn how to watch what I think around you."

Finn gave her only a crooked grin in return, but his permission boosted her boldness. This time, she was in control. She reached up a hand to his face and brushed a smudge of dirt off his cheek. She pushed a lock of hair behind his ear, letting her fingers trail down the rough line of his jaw. She cupped the side of his face and, gently, leaned in and placed her lips on his. Like their hiding place, the kiss was secret, and safe, and sweet as the moonlight. When he kissed her back, Kai's heart soared.

When they finally came up for air, Finn threw back his head and let out a long, cathartic, almost joyous howl that echoed through the forest. Kai laughed and howled with him. As she did, her hand flew unconsciously to her throat, where her mati remained, unbroken.

ACKNOWLEDGEMENTS

Huge thanks to Kristen Painter for creating this fabulous town…and then inviting me to play in her world. Kristen had especially perfect timing—I'd just come home sick from a conference and was mainlining *Lost Girl* on Netflix when I got the email about the launch of her Nocturne Falls Universe. I pretty much dropped every project I had going on at the time just to write this book. (I made sure to give her full credit, too, every time I missed a deadline.) I also blamed her for the fact that I craved chocolate *the whole time*.

Double-huge thanks to my Brute Squad and my Dragon Con family, who have met up with me every Labor Day weekend for the past twenty years, in Atlanta, in costume. They've spent days and night and literally paraded around the city with me…and they continue to inspire me online for the entire rest of the year. I do believe that Dragon Con is the closest thing anyone will ever experience to Nocturne Falls in real life, and I am honored to say that I was raised there.

And triple-huge thanks to my Big Fat Greek family, who raised me in a world steeped with as much tradition as superstition. I will never toast with water, I will always spit or knock wood to avoid accidentally cursing someone, and I wear my mati with pride. Much love especially to my little sister, Soteria, and my mom and dad—Marcy and George Kontis—who live right down the street from me, and I am so very, very happy that they do. My life, and my writing, would not be the same without them.

ABOUT THE AUTHOR

New York Times and *USA Today* bestselling author Alethea Kontis is a princess, a fairy godmother, and a geek. She's known for screwing up the alphabet, making horror movies with her friends, and ranting about fairy tales on YouTube.

Alethea's published works include novels, novellas, and companions in the universes of Arilland, Nocturne Falls, Barefoot Bay, and Sherrilyn Kenyon's Dark-Hunters; the AlphaOops picture books; *Haven, Kansas; Wild & Wishful, Dark & Dreaming*; *The Wonderland Alphabet;* and *Diary of a Mad Scientist Garden Gnome*. Her short fiction, essays, and poetry have appeared in a myriad of anthologies and magazines.

Alethea's YA fairy tale novel, *Enchanted*, won both the Gelett Burgess Children's Book Award and Garden State Teen Book Award. *Enchanted* was nominated for the Audie Award in 2013 and was selected for World Book Night in 2014. Both *Enchanted* and its sequel, *Hero*, were nominated for the Andre Norton Award. *Tales of Arilland*, a short story collection set in the same fairy tale world, won a second Gelett Burgess Award in 2015. The second book in The Trix Adventures, *Trix and the Faerie Queen*, was a finalist for the Dragon Award in 2016.

Princess Alethea was given the honor of speaking about fairy tales at the Library of Congress in 2013. In 2015, she gave a keynote address at the Lewis Carroll Society's Alice150 Conference in New York City, celebrating the 150th anniversary of *Alice's Adventures in Wonderland*. She also enjoys speaking at schools and festivals all over the US. (If forced to choose between all these things, she says middle schools are her favorite!)

Born in Burlington, Vermont, Alethea currently lives and writes on the Space Coast of Florida. She makes the best baklava you've ever tasted and sleeps with a teddy bear named Charlie. Find out more about Princess Alethea and the magic, wonderful world in which she lives here: https://www.patreon.com/princessalethea

ALSO BY ALETHEA KONTIS

Want to know when Alethea has a new book out?
Sign up for the newsletter! You'll receive periodic
emails about new releases, book sales, Princess
Alethea merchandise, and videos featuring the
author princess herself!
Sign up today: http://eepurl.com/YSmS1